FESTIVAL of FOOLS

About *Kelly:* a novel by Michael Mullen

for Liam McLoughlin, friend
and for Breda Lemoine, Paris

Books by Michael Mullen
Kelly: a Novel (Wolfhound Press 1981)
Festival of Fools (Wolfhound Press 1984)
Magus the Lollipop Man (Canongate 1981; Wolfhound 1983)
Sea Wolves From The North (Wolfhound Press 1983)

FESTIVAL of FOOLS

Michael Mullen

WOLFHOUND PRESS

07807229

First published by
WOLFHOUND PRESS
68 Mountjoy Square, Dublin 1.

British Library Cataloguing in Publication Data

Mullen, Michael
    Festival of fools.
    1. Title
    823'. 914[F]   PR6063.U38/

ISBN 0-905473-91-4
ISBN 0-86327-051-4 Pbk.

Cover illustration by Keggy Carew
Cover typography: Michael O'Brien
Typesetting by Print Prep Limited, Dublin.
Printed and bound by Billings & Sons Ltd.

This book is published with the assistance of
The Arts Council (An Chomhairle Ealaíon),
Dublin, Ireland.

CHAPTER ONE

Inis Orga was double-humped like a Bactrian camel. It rested upon a sullen sea. To the east lay the municipal town of Baile. To the south lay the sea route to Byzantium.

Tostach Joyce looked out from his cottage upon the day. Light was dead on the waves. The morning was smudged into grey masses of colour. No wind stirred in the east. The island would be free from the stench of the offal heap which corrupted above Baile.

——Thanks to the ministering angels who shunt the winds this way and that and throw the seas into confusion, I won't have the rot from the hill on the walls of my throat, he said in orison from the luxurious depths of the Great French Whore's bed.

Grim rain fell upon the island. It had fallen before Tostach was born, and on the day he was born, and it would rain on the day when they carried his anchorite flesh to the graveyard. Sucking at his pipe above a regal quilt he looked out at the drizzle.

——It will wear down the world in the end, he commented to himself.

'You should take a woman into the house,' the poets of the island had told him once when they gathered for the court of poetry. 'Take a woman into the house?' he had cried. 'Men have died before their time from marriage.' 'It's not a good thing to be alone,' they had said, taking thoughtful pipes from their mouths and spitting philosophical saliva into the ashes. 'I'm never alone. I have stories and images inside my head which keep me company on the long rainy days and the bitter winter nights.' 'The flesh never stings?' 'No. It only stings when the rheumatism puts its teeth into my hips now and then.' That was before he discovered the

5

Great French Whore's bed.

The feather bed was his only large possession. It was as wide as the sea, soft as moss, deep as contentment in the belly after porter. It carried the escutcheons of the House of Orleans on the headboard and the finely-carved body of Venus on the endboard. Floating in oak, she looked up at him with eternal invitation in her lines. The figure of the Greek goddess engendered Continental temptations in his Celtic imagination. He often spoke to her by dull tallow light, exploring her lines with a toe rimmed by a cuticle of dirt. Above this nest of luxury a Tiepolo fresco opened into an Arcadian sky, full of foreign blues and greens. On puffy clouds gods and goddesses reclined in eternal ease.

— I suppose it's the largest bed in the world, he said often to himself as he sucked at his clay pipe. None of the subjects of Queen Victoria have sleeping quarters like it. Looking up at the painted sky a man could easily think that this was no bed at all, but the bottom of a distant world without a catechism.

He couldn't believe his eyes, the day he saw it bobbing up and down like a large lobster pot. That was the morning after the great storm which brought no good to anybody. And there upon the top of it lay the man from Africa, his mouth full of saltwater and seaweed. It is strange what the sea will throw up, he thought. He mused long about it as he had very little else to do.

The carved Venus was the first naked woman he had ever looked upon in his life. He studied her carefully, as artists study pictures on varnishing day. He could not call her brazen, like one might call the Nestor woman brazen. She had a confident look in her eye and nakedness was natural to her, as slates are to a roof, and crowns to kings. The bed-panel was scattering seeds of damnation across his mind. Wickedness which had been theological was now both real and full of luxury.

The man from Africa dried out in the sun and groaned in Swahili. He heaved out the last of saltwater and turned on his back.

He could father piebald giants, Tostach Joyce thought to himself. It was a great day for thought.

The black man, an Adam-within-the-walls, rose from the sand. He stood dazed.

Tostach, with the stem of his pipe, directed him towards

an ass. Sack-strewn on the ass's back, Tostach carried him to
the cottage on a small ledge above the sea and protected by
sour hills. Here he stood him up by the door and went inside.
He rummaged in a mahogany chest and emerged with a large
army trousers and a red army coat he had stripped from a
drowned soldier, and then gave it to the man from Africa,
whose skin in bright light was deep and purple. Tostach
pulled an imaginary pair of trousers over his own rough
ones and indicated that the man should follow his actions.
Then he mimed that he should put on the red coat and do
up the gold buttons. Although they were two sizes too small
for him they did protect him from the cold and the damp.

It took them two days to get the bed up from the beach
and into the house. They had to knock down a side wall and
breach the thatch to do it. But the man possessed great
strength and ability, and so he rebuilt the wall and patched
the roof. The house was now about the bed.

When Tostach Joyce lay between the French sheets for
the first time and sank his backside into the mattress of pea-
cock down, his sensatory nerves almost shattered with delight.
He twisted and turned like a dissipated pasha tickled with
ostrich plumes.

—You can be too comfortable sometimes, he said to the
man from Africa, who did not understand him. So comfortable that it can be painful.

They lay in bed together and gazed up at the canopy. It
was like looking through a hole in the thatch and a gap in
the stars, into a circular world peopled by secular gods. Whoever painted that had a great gift and a pagan mind, Tostach
thought. The great work above his head was a wonder to be
taken slowly and in parts, like a poem.

—There is no single thing out of place. There are gods
where there should be gods and empty spaces where there
should be empty spaces, and not like a confusion of cattle a
man would see on a fair day.

A week he spent in the bed. Each night he was visited by
European thoughts, damnable and multicoloured. After a
week he decided to put on his trousers and get some sun.

He sat a whole day in his *sugán* chair at the eastern end of
the house, trying to decide upon an appropriate name for the
drift-flesh carried into the bay. It was a difficult task. He took
a serious pride in his choice of words. He was as rigid in his
judgement as governors of art galleries. He tested the ring of
each name for crack or fault. All day it eluded him in the

stubble of his imagination. The sun was retracting its commit-
ment to the day when he hit upon Pádraigh Gorm na Mara,
or Purple Pat from the Sea. It was as finely-wrought as a
haiku and had the sleek resilience of a currach. Above all, it
carried sincerity and truth. He went indoors, threw turf on
the fire, boiled potatoes and fish and drank milk. He was
pleased with his day of thought. He had composed a small
poem with image equal to object.

He sat in front of the fire with the man from Africa and
said to him several times ——Pádraigh Gorm na Mara.

The purple man made many attempts before he mastered
his first syllables in Irish. But soon he knew his name and,
pointing to himself, said —— Pádraigh Gorm na Mara.

Then Tostach Joyce thought that it would be wise to
teach him his own name so he pointed to his chest and said
——Tostach.

——Tostach.

Thus began Pádraigh's introduction to the Irish language.

Later Tostach said in Irish ——Hand me down the fiddle,
and pointed in the general direction of the mantlepiece.

·Pádraigh Gorm na Mara took down a framed oleograph
of Saint Patrick. Tostach shook his head. Pádraigh reached
for a clay pipe. Tostach shook his head again. Finally after
many mistakes he took down the fiddle, a gift from the
treacherous sea and made by Stradivarius Cremonensis in 1717.

Tostach tuned the fiddle with ceremony and marshalled
the five strings into concordance. Then, viceing it under his
chin, he began to play. Pádraigh Gorm na Mara listened
attentively, his ears unaccustomed to the sound. After some
time he took down the *bowrán* from the mantlepiece and
counterpointed Tostach's music with African rhythms. Then
he stood in the space between bed and fire and started dancing. Tostach had never witnessed such antics in his life. He
placed the fiddle on the nob of his knee and let the purple
man tap out the rhythms which were pounding within him.
The beating and stamping grew louder and filled the house
and the valley. Finally it took on the noise and tempo of
the sea.

——There is some devil inside his soul, eating him, and if
I had any sense I would have no truck with the powers of
blackness and darkness, for it will all come to no good in the
end, like weather under a disturbed moon.

Pádraigh Gorm na Mara danced out through the door and
down the steep path to the sea and along the sand. Tostach

followed. He was in a death sweat like Tostach had seen on
the corpses of troubled souls who had struggled against the
lieutenants of death. The voice of the African disturbed the
cycle of peace about the island. The seals took to the waves;
the sea gulls circled and cried, pricking the darkness with their
calls. In a final gesture Pádraigh whirled about, screeched in
ecstasy and fell on the sand.

There are two kinds of darkness, Tostach thought. One is
the blackness of the night, the other the blackness of the
soul, and this is the latter and I should have nothing to do
with it. I'll leave bad enough alone. I'll let the powers of good
and the powers of evil struggle for his soul. So he lit his pipe
and listened to the sea now mellowed and looked up at the
stars back in their constant orbits.

The purple man was breathing quietly in a deep sleep.
Sweat phosphored on his body, and he shone like a silver
dolphin beached by the waves.

Pádraigh Gorm na Mara woke. He had been exorcised of
some African devil. He followed Tostach back to the cottage
and they went to sleep in the Great French Whore's bed,
backside to backside and in deep Continental luxury.

The newcomer was a quick learner and an eager apprentice.
Tostach carried out his straw chair and introduced him to the
rudiments of Irish island culture. He concentrated on the fifty
basic Celtic survival words, pointing out each noun with his
stick. Sea, sky, bog, rock, boat, fish, milk, tea, potato and
peeler were the first Irish words which Pádraigh mastered.
Tostach knew that they were essential if he were to survive
on the scab of land above the sea. Later he introduced him
to the active verbs: dig, fish, milk, kindle, eat, and run like
hell. Soon Pádraigh Gorm na Mara had conquered his first
simple Irish words.

Not only was his mind sharp and bright, but also he had
agile hands which could work the land and harvest the sea.
He acquired the skills of the island. He could dig potatoes,
pick them clean from the soil and bury the stalks to replenish
famished earth. He learned how to pit potatoes, insulating
them with straw from the frost. His two pits were neat and
straight and looked like the graves of two unknown soldiers.
He also took easily to milking the cow, Caileach Crosta. He
seduced milk out of her and his fingers were like the talk of
a wastrel trying to inveigle money out of a rich widow. It
flowed out in torrents, giving more in milk than she had
taken in grass. Pádraigh Gorm na Mara creeled the turf home

from the mountains in August and built it into a neat stack at
the gable end of the house. He stole the secret of thatching
from Faber Dowling by sitting on a ditch and observing
every clever move he made. He painted the door and windows of the cottage red and coated the walls in white lime
ground from shells. He carried driftwood from the beach on
his broad shoulders and built two sheds, one for Caileach
Crosta and her new calf, the other for farm implements and
tools. Pádraigh learned currach craft and the secrets of the
sea. He put on rough trousers and a sweater with the symbols
of the island knitted into it so that his body might be returned
to Inis Orga if it were washed up on a strange shore.

After this fashion Pádraigh Gorm na Mara, shipwrecked on
the edge of Europe, thrown up by a troubled sea, found a
new master in Tostach Joyce and settled down to the tranquil
and slow-rhythmed life of Inis Orga.

—I'll stay here for ever, Pádraigh Gorm na Mara told
Tostach Joyce when he gained fluency in the Irish language.

—Stay until the plug is pulled out of the bottom of the
sea, Tostach told him from the luxury of his bed.

—It will be a rest from my journeys, for I have been servant and slave from the Pillars of Hercules to the shores of
Byzantium. It's a long story.

—Hold it for the winter months when there is no work
outside and we are all driven indoors. Then, fancy gives
warmth and light.

The kettle, furred with black, hung from the iron crook
over the fire. The lid spluttered and chattered. Pádraigh Gorm
na Mara swung out the crook with a potato bag and poured
five large spoons of tea into the boiling water.

—You are becoming a dab hand at making the tea.

—I have a good teacher.

—Like all arts, it needs practice.

Pádraigh took two enamel mugs from their hooks under
the mantlepiece, scalded them and poured in the tea. Then he
sweetened them with brown sugar, a drift-gift from the sea,
and laced them with poteen. He buttered a soda-cake quarter
with strong homemade butter. He carried the bread and the
tea to the bed and slid in beside Tostach Joyce. They sipped
the tea with discrimination and ate the bread, chewing it
slowly, calculating the time of the day from the window light.

—I think I'll stay on in bed today, Pádraigh.

—I'll haul the lobster pots and bring the turf down from
the hill.

——Since you drifted ashore you have taken a lot of bother off my mind. My fancy is free and this bed is equal in content to the fields of heaven.

——Take your ease, Tostach.

——Indeed I will, and a wooden Venus at the base of my bed.

——I saw the lights of Baile last night when the mist cleared.

——Baile is a foreign country, as strange as that Byzantium where you served and slaved. If there is sense in Baile it belongs to Noah McNulty, who is building a large boat which will take him to some foreign city. I must show it to you sometime or other. The rest are mad, by any standards but their own.

——You chew a lot of inward grass, Tostach.

——Thought suits me.

They returned to their tea-sipping. They rolled the brown wash about in their mouths.

——Indian tea, I would say, Tostach mused.

——I'd place it in Ceylon.

They wanted for nothing as they looked down at Venus and up at the Tiepolo sky-people.

——I've been thinking, Tostach.

——About what?

——Money.

——There is no money to be made around here, or that crowd from Baile would have thought about it in that gut-festering town.

——Well, I have picked up a few Irish proverbs since I came to the island and, as you said, there is hidden wisdom in such proverbs. There is one which says that what is unusual is amazing, and another which says that there are long horns on cattle over the sea. We have three things on this island which could be regarded as amazing or made amazing.

——And what could be made amazing in this island? Tostach Joyce asked.

——Poteen. Its potential has not been exploited.

——Yes. The natural island drink by others could be regarded as amazing. We are impressed at this lateral thinking.

——We have lobsters. They are deviants and do not follow normal evolutionary trends.

——You have read Darwin then?

——Yes.

——Go on. We continue to be impressed.

——Oysters.

——I hate oysters. They are slugs in salt water.

——They may be to you. I have seen them on the plates of queens.

——They may be amazing but they are not amazing enough.

——Let us spread the rumour that they are aphrodisiacs.

——What are aphrodisiacs?

——It's derived from the word Aphrodite. And he explained the word further.

——Well, I'll be damned, Tostach Joyce told him when Pádraigh Gorm na Mara had finished. If we could spread such a rumour, and people will believe anything, then men would dive down to the bottom of the sea and eat oysters raw.

——We could fill the barn with gold. ——And buy ten cows.

——And a white horse. ——And a good serge, Sunday suit.

——I have thought of all that while pulling the lobster pots. I also thought that I might say that I came ashore as an African pygmy, and that having eaten the lobsters I grew to huge proportions.

——A good rumour to spread! But it will be hard to adjust, for we have been miserable here in the island for so long, we take it as natural. A patch on the backside of your coat and on your elbow is more natural than no patch.

——The patterns of thought may be changed. Gold is a great changer of things.

——I'll have to put all this before the School of Poetry when it assembles.

——What School of Poetry?

——It's no secret, all Baile knows. Come November, there is no poet on the island of Inis Orga but gathers in here with the verses he has composed during the summer. I'm the head poet. I've written and composed many verses in my day. When I'm dead and in a thousand years from now, if the island can withstand the wear of the rain and the tear of the sea, they will be reciting the verses of Tostach Joyce's poetry.

——Give us a poem.

——I will. It's an occasional piece about an ass which died on me. I have to chant it so you can get the full value of it on your ear. Here it is.

> I had an ass none could surpass
> Who weathered every storm.
> There was no ass, which ate green grass,
> To equal him for form.
> He did no harm about the farm

And what he did was good.
With a charm to cause alarm
He carried turf and wood.
And now I say on New Year's Day,
The hills with snow were clad,
He ate bad hay and that put pay
To the finest ass I had.

—You thought highly of that ass.

—I did not. He was bone-lazy and no good to anyone, but when he died I had to glorify him. That is the right of every poet.

—I see.

—I bet you didn't see how well I used internal rhymes in the poem.

—No. Poetry is beyond me.

—That's what you must look out for. Anything else is rubbish. It took me two months to write that poem.

—Well, nobody would suspect you were a poet.

—The Irish poet is a steeplechaser with a jennet's hide and to look at him you wouldn't suspect quality. He keeps a manged cow, drinks milk, burns wet turf in his hearth, and is humped over grey ashes like a soul straying in limbo, but within he has regal quality, a prince, you might say, covered with jewels.

To Pádraigh Gorm na Mara — who had been to jewelled places, in marble Muslim palaces, had slept upon the down of red flamingoes, and had been outward — it was a foreign land, this inward land of Tostach Joyce, centrally-heated and gold-brightened by the imagination.

They had no more to say. Tostach Joyce slid down beneath the royal sheets and Pádraigh went to pull the lobster pots.

November was a sullen month on Inis Orga. The island closed in upon itself. Curtains of rain fell on grey seas and stirred muddy sediment in the blood. The wind, uncertain and twisted, carried rheumatic messages and pessimism. That was the reason why the poets went inwards.

It was during these incestuous months that the culture of Inis Orga flourished, grew strong, and purged itself of foreign words which might have made their way into their cultural blood during the summer. It was a time when the poets became possessed by the spirits of the old poets who spoke through their brittle bodies. The tea and poteen were transmuted into mead and wine. Bread became kingfood. The winds threw a rampart about the island. There were no Danemarauding tribulations.

They had earned the disrespect of Baile because they spent their time shaping proverbs, and tuning them to the correct verbal pitch.

—Eventually they will die out, the townspeople commented. The Queen's English they know only in a fragmented form. Each one of them thinks he is of royal blood and has ancestors among the demi-Irish gods. They are stubborn and inward, Christian only in the top layers of their hearts. Out there they go to bed for five months and live on potatoes.

They let the rain draw a gestatory cawl about the island.

On the first day of November the bardic school convened in Tostach Joyce's cottage. As they came by twisted and treeless roads communal fire began to burn in their hearts. By the time they reached the cottage they were word-drunk and warm.

They formed a chapel of fifteen: Tostach Joyce, Long John, Pat and Pagan, Gub Keogh, Duck Flaherty, Stone Ryan, Turf Gilpin, Mackerel Malone, Kipper Padden, Celibate Corcoran, Amorous Aynsworth, Stitcher Sweeney, The Yellow Gunner, Cramp Carney, Rigmarole Rodgers.

They came like moths to a fire. Tostach Joyce's house was well-stocked with poetic provisions: potatoes, oatmeal, butter, flour, fourteen sides of bacon, fifteen barrels of poteen, soda-bread cakes and turf.

They were surprised to find Tostach Joyce in bed. They were more surprised to find that the bed was one of great magnitude and finish. They were more surprised still to discover that Pádraigh Gorm na Mara, who wet the tea for them, could speak fluent Irish.

They sat around the comfortable bed and looked in at Tostach, an island in a sea of comfort, cap on head and pipe in mouth.

—Not being curious, Tostach, but how did you come by the large bed and your man from Africa? Rigmarole Rodgers asked.

—Floating in the sea after a great storm, on the bed, replied Tostach, and he told them the story.

—There is nothing like it in the island annals, Gub Keogh said.

—I know. The tide's turn surely brings wonders.

—It must be the largest bed in Christendom, Duck

Flaherty said.

—And the largest bed in Pagandom, for the curved and carved lady would suggest that it came, perhaps, from the East, Pat the Pagan suggested.

—Well, wherever it came from, it's here.

—If a man took off his trousers on a windy November day like today and got into it, he wouldn't stir until the soft winds of June were blowing, Stitcher Sweeney said.

—A regiment would fit in it, The Yellow Gunner observed.

—I'd give a bag of potatoes to spend a night in it, Amorous Aynsworth said.

—Sure, take off your trousers and come in, eight on top and seven at the bottom, like rashers on a pan.

They took off their trousers and hung them on the nails behind the door and entered Byzantium. Its comfort stung them. They oo'ed and aa'd with burning pleasure. Their wind-and-rain-hardened bodies soon succumbed to the regal pleasure of the down mattress.

—Pádraigh Gorm, Tostach said, make more tea and cut the curranty cake you made.

Soon fifteen pipes, under fifteen caps, puffed thoughtful smoke. They drank tea charged with poteen. When they began to eat the curranty cake their nerve systems were almost on overload.

—Would you like to make easy money? Tostach asked.

—We would. How could we make easy money? they asked communally.

While Tostach told them pipe smoke scarfed and eeled about the rafters and drifted down and out through the chimney.

—You know, if we made that sort of money, we would never have to leave this bed until the ribs of the world rotted, Cramp Carney said.

—We could make poetry until the final tide ran out, Turf Gilpin added.

—You better start the rumour, Pádraigh, and let it grow, they all said.

The clouds settled on the mountains. The wind cut bone deep. There was sparse movement on Aisling pier. Currachs, black backed, wintered on the beach.

In Tostach Joyce's cottage, under French sheets, the school of poetry opened.

It had been a good year for verse. The sun had been warm, there was honey in the heather, bird song had been clear.

At the extreme corner of the bed, his mind rattled with drink, lay The Yellow Gunner.

—When he's not drinking, he's thinking of drink. It will kill him.

He had spent the summer travelling the roads of Ireland playing a tin whistle for coppers. Each year in mid-October he felt the call of the island.

—What have you to show after a year's work? they asked.

—Words and ideas, but I can't match them.

—And what is the poem about?

—A yellow bittern.

—Nobody ever wrote a poem about a yellow bittern. It's hardly a fit subject for poetry. The eagle, the robin, the lark and the blackbird, yes. But not a bittern, Gub Keogh told him.

—I look to those in nature who are like myself.

—Well, tell us the run of it then.

—I'll try.

—One day in winter, coming from Gort, I saw a dead bittern on a frozen lake. It disturbed me more than the Sack of Troy for it had died from the lack of drink. I said it was terrible that one who loved drink so well died for the want of it. I decided then and there to drink while I can.

—That type of conclusion is immoral, Mackerel Malone said.

—Poetry is neither moral nor immoral, Tostach Joyce said firmly. Let him continue.

—Soon the rats will come to my wake, I thought. I weep for one like myself. I'll drink while I can, for I can't wet a lip dead, Gunner said.

—It's a controversial poem, Celibate Corcoran commented.

—It's honest, Tostach told him.

—That's the first time anybody mentioned honesty as a quality of poetry, Cramp Carney said. None of the bards ever held that.

—Well, I'm holding it, Tostach Joyce said firmly.

—The poem came out of a scattered mind, Turf Gilpin added.

—And so it should, Tostach told them. Poems of hard grain come from darkness, doubt, and the fear we have of life, and the greater fear we have of death.

—Last year you held different views.

—I wasn't thinking last year, and I'm having serious doubts if the poem about my ass is as great as I formerly thought. We have argued too much. Let us fall into a poetic sleep.

They lay back, lit their pipes, looked upwards at the Greek sky. Then a strange thing happened: their spirits levitated, each standing above its body, a transparent replica of a poet. Together they ascended towards the Tiepolo painting. When they reached the canvas they lost a dimension, took on a Renaissance pigmentation and became part of the picture.

Pádraigh Gorm na Mara watched their ascension into heaven.

—Celtic Ireland is certainly an eventful and wonderful place, he said to himself. These Irish are the greatest dreamers ever created and can change winter into summer by taking asylum in the landscapes of their imagination.

He looked at the fifteen corpses on the bed. They were ripe for a wake but not for a burial.

Tostach Joyce was the first spirit to drag himself through the floor of Tiepolo's heaven, perhaps because he was the chief of poets, perhaps because his spirit was more refined. The rest followed through with ease or difficulty, depending on the grossness or clarity of their souls.

They discovered changes in their bodies which surprised them in many ways. They could now move at the speed of thought across the span of Attic sky; they could pass unhindered through matter; skin bloomed, flesh softened; virility passed through Amorous Aynsworth's loins; gapped teeth filled, uneven teeth straightened, tobacco-stained teeth whitened; bald patches were rethatched; all had been given the gift of Greek.

Many things remained unchanged. They still wore their longjohns and carried their caps upon their heads. They continued to smoke their pipes. They had their mugs of poteen in their hands. Their natures had not become more or less virtuous.

—You could get fine potatoes and turnips from this land, Stitcher Sweeney told them, letting fine, red earth sieve through his fingers.

They studied the sun-drenched soil and spat out brown saliva on the tawny grass. They raised their eyes from the grass to the baked landscape and to the mountains.

—I see they have no stone walls. We must be on commonage, Pat the Pagan said.

They had come to rest in the shade of a vine. Mackerel Malone plucked a bunch of dark red grapes and ate some.

—Eat these, he said. They are five-and-a-half times sweeter than blackberries.

They blooded their mouths with grape juice and rested under the noon pool of vine shadows.

By now The Yellow Gunner had disappeared. He had smelt wine on the air. He wine-wished and found himself sitting in a scoop of chalk-rock with Bacchus.

Bacchus, bloated, looked at him in surprise, his lips heavy with wine.

—Who are you? Bacchus asked.

—The Yellow Gunner.

—And what are you doing here?

—What I was doing before I arrived, drinking. And he drank from his bottle of poteen, which he had grabbed prior to levitation.

—Liquor from the grape? Bacchus asked.

—No, from the barley.

—May I partake?

—I'll barter with you. I'll give you the remainder of the bottle for two barrels of wine.

—Done! said Bacchus. He stood up, breathing heavily inside his soft garments. He went into his cave and rolled out two barrels of wine.

The Gunner tapped the barrel, let flow a spout of wine into a mug and plugged the hole. He drank a large cool mouthful.

—There is sun in it and long warm days, he said, looking at the Attic hills.

Bacchus put the bottle of poteen to his mouth and gulped a mouthful.

—Oh! It's warm stuff. It comes from a cold country. There is rain and heather in it, short days and long nights, turf fires and outrageous stories.

The Gunner sucked the taste of wine from between his new teeth and, although he could have been anywhere else in Greece that he wished, he remained where he was.

—Would you like to hear a story?

—Yes, said Bacchus. I'd love to hear a good story.

—Do you know what a yellow bittern is, by any chance?

—No.

—Well, I'll tell you then. I was a gunner to the Queen and

one day, coming home drunk, by a frozen lake I saw a dead
bird, a yellow bittern. And from that beginning he continued.

Bacchus was all gasps of wonder, putting aside his bottle
now and then to exclaim:

—You don't tell me now! and By the backside of Apollo!
or You're having me on!

—Upon my soul, but no word of a lie. I saw it all one
morning in winter, staggering home drunk. It sobered me up
and I made a promise to myself that I would drink while I
had time left.

—A worthy decision.

—My whole life is in that story, if only I could shape it
into a poem. Some say it will be immoral.

—Damn the begrudgers. It's the likes of them who plug
up the wine barrels of pleasure and laughter. We could well
do without their company. You know, you're a great little
man.

—Thanks. It's good to be endorsed.

—And don't worry about the poem. It will come, and
when it does it will last forever.

—But it's not written.

—Time, Gunner. Leave the mind open. I remember once
a fellow called Homer. He was lame and blind. He travelled
the country for years saying that he would write a great poem.

—Did he?

—He did.

—We'll drink to Homer.

They did.

—I'd like to spend time on Inis Orga.

—Can you fish and compose poetry?

—No.

—Well, you would be no use there.

They left it at that.

The Gunner had no particular thought in his head when
the first line of the poem came to him. But come it did, like
the first bonham from a sow, blue-veined and cold. He cleaned
the slime from it and there it was, pounding after life. Line
after line came, like bonham after bonham out of a dark sow's
belly. And then the poem had littered.

—I have it. I have it, he danced, and there never has been
a poem like it.

He canted it out and it went immediately into a Greek
translation.

—You have it surely, Bacchus said, and joined in a dance

with him.

——You have given me great wine and great heart, Bacchus.

——We will go in search of more wine.

With the arm of Bacchus on The Gunner's shoulder and The Gunner's arm around the left cheek of Bacchus' bum, they staggered across the landscape, swilling each other's drink, The Yellow Gunner impotent but filled with lecherous desire, as poets and writers are after creation.

Stone Ryan spat red grape pips into the soil between his splayed feet and wondered who was the best stonemason in Greece.

He found himself by a marble quarry. A swarthy Greek with a spade beard stood at the quarry mouth, supervising a group of workmen chiselling grooves into marble drums, barrel-tall.

——Have you come for a job? Phidias asked.

——No. I was passing the road and the hammering caught my ear. I am a mason myself.

——How many temples have you built?

——I built a cathedral once for a bishop, he lied.

——I'm Phidias.

——I'm Stone Ryan.

Satisfied that his men were gainfully employed, Phidias took mallet and chisel and started to work on a half-finished statue.

——That's a fine bit of work, but you are chiselling the clothes off her. If you continue she'll end up naked. If I were to carve a statue like that I'd be excommunicated.

——Nobody notices here. Most people walk around naked.

——Is that the law?

——No, it's the custom. Did you ever try your hand at a statue?

——No. I'm a tombstone and celtic cross mason.

——It's a morbid occupation. I prefer to carve the strong, the perfect and the beautiful.

——I'd love to try my hand.

——Try. Take a chisel and a mallet. You carve one breast and I'll carve another. Don't chip off a nipple with a loose stroke. A drunk apprentice of mine once knocked off the arms of one of the finest statues I ever carved, of a lady down at Milo.

——I'll be careful.

They stood before the statue and looked for breasts concealed within the stone. They worked in silence, and for a long time. The day passed. At evening it was time to rest. They rubbed the marble dust from their eyes and sat down.

—Do you think you have mastered the art of statue making?

—I think I have. Is there anything I could give you in return?

—I've taken a fancy to your cap and your clay pipe.

—They're yours, Stone Ryan said, and he gave them to Phidias.

—Thanks, Stone. You can have the mallet, chisel and statue in exchange. And remember the strokes.

—I never forget a stroke.

They let the cool air of Attica dry the sweat from under their armpits.

Rigmarole Rodgers found himself sitting in an empty amphitheatre. Below him in the deep-welled space a serious figure, sucking a pebble, beat the stubborn air with his clenched hand.

He stopped and looked up at Rigmarole.

—Who are you? —Rodgers. Rigmarole Rodgers. —Are you a barbarian? —No, an islandman. I'm from Inis Orga. —Is it beyond the Pillars of Hercules? —I don't know. It's beyond Ireland. —Did you like my speech? —As good as any parish priest. —I'm defending democracy. —Is democracy worth defending? —It is. Is Inis Orga a democracy? —I don't know. —Have you freedom of speech? —Yes. —Well, you live in a democracy. How is Ireland? —The most disgraceful country that ever yet was seen. —I'll go over the speech again and be on the look-out for weak patches. My name is Demosthenes. —Demosthenes what? —Plain Demosthenes.

Tostach Joyce was sitting on a stone bench, smoking his pipe, in the house of Cephalos. He listened to a group of men discuss the state of affairs and the affairs of state.

—Who are you? asked a small, pugg-faced man with bowed legs and skin rough from exposure to the wind.

—Tostach Joyce.

—I'm Socrates. Are you in search of wisdom?

—I am, if it is to be found.

—If you like what we say, good and well. If you disagree, say so and we will argue further. We seek truth here.

——A most difficult thing to find.

Tostach liked Socrates. He was always asking questions, taking sentences apart and putting them together in another way, and always making them more clear than they originally were. Each word was like a sod in a good clamp of turf. Tostach would have spent a long time here but the symposium was disturbed by the voice of a woman.

——Socrates. Socrates, she called.

——It's Xanthippe, they said.

——I'd better run for it, Socrates told them. He gathered his Greek raiment about him and fled.

——That woman is a shrew, they all said. She never gives the man any peace.

Meanwhile, Amorous Aynsworth's desires were ripening in the sun, like fat American corn. He was standing at a crossroads in a grove of laurel. A woman rushed past.

——Not a bloody screed on her, he remarked.

Another dashed past.

——Not a bloody screed on her either. It must be the custom here, and who am I to break customs.

Naked and primed, he rushed from the place ——I'm free, he called, I'm free. Nobody knows me and I can do what I want.

He did. All day long among the green laurels and upon moss he went ——oo oh! and the women went ——aa ah! and he went ——ee eh! and they went ——ii iii! and they all went ——uu uh! together. At the end of the day he was as weak as Doran's bull after congress. He doubted if he would ever write poetry again.

Each of the poets satisfied his Greek desires. They satisfied them through a long day and longer evenings in a landscape of sun, burnt grass, wines, marble columns, philosophers, builders, poets and bacchants.

A week later, to the very hour, the spirits came through the floor of the picture. They descended into inert bodies. They began to stir with life.

The poets carried back more than memories. The Gunner had a barrel of wine and his poem. Stone Ryan a chisel, a mallet and a half-finished statue. Amorous Aynsworth returned longjohnless.

——Travel broadens the mind, Amorous Aynsworth said.

And customs change from place to place. The fact that we are Celtic, and covered, does not necessarily mean that all others are.

——By the way, they asked him, where are your longjohns?

——A Greek stole them. I ran after him and he wore me out.

——The Greeks make good wine, The Yellow Gunner told them, his keg of wine upright at the corner of the bed.

A lonely wind troubled the thatch and cried in the neck of the flue. It ran across the hills, tearing its starved belly on whins and brown ferns.

——It will be a lonesome winter, Cramp Carney said. There is no call to stir from beneath these blankets until the days grow long and the buds split.

——Agreed, agreed, agreed, the true voice of democracy, they spoke as one.

——It's equal to me. We have enough to eat, but hardly enough to smoke, said Tostach.

——Don't worry about smoking. Five crates of American tobacco have been washed up on Barra Strand! I brought them up in the ass and creels, rejoined Pádraigh.

——Well, if we have enough tobacco, then we can rest here for the winter.

They asked Pádraigh Gorm na Mara how the rumour was spreading. He told them that while they were away he had walked across the hills to Aisling pier, a sailor's cap on his head, a heavy coat buttoned across his chest and several languages on his tongue. He said that in snug corners around fires he told the foreign sailors of the lobsters of Inish Orga, how they carried beneath their red armour and white shields a flesh with potency beyond measure.

——Many of the young women in this island are well over a hundred, he told the sailors.

——It's a hard thing to believe, they muttered to themselves in Arabic and French.

——We do not wish it to be known outside the island. It's a great secret. And our poteen keeps men young and manly well into their hundred and twenties.

——Tell us more.

——I was four feet when I came to the island one hundred years ago. I had to stop eating the oysters.

The foreign sailors stayed their pints and imagined. Their wives were young again in France and Arabia; they themselves had the power of stallions.

——I alone know where the oysters are. The secret has been handed on to me by Tostach Joyce, who has been excommuniated, even by the Church of Byzantium.

——We've heard of him. He sleeps in the Great French Whore's bed. It is said that he has not put on his trousers to turn a hand since the day he felt the comfort of the big mattress.

——Lies. All lies. He's young enough to be his eldest son. Women are coming from all over the island, carrying butter and eggs, to sleep in that bed of his.

While the sailors were masticating these facts he took a poteen bottle from his pocket and uncorked it.

——I'm feeling weak, he said, and herein lies my strength.

He put the bottle to his mouth and drank evenly. He palmed the cork back on the bottle and said ——I could knot iron.

He took a horseshoe from over the fireplace and straightened it out. Then he put a knot on it.

——That's what poteen does for me. I'm not feeling as well as I should. Normally I unknot it.

CHAPTER TWO

The harbour town of Baile faced the sea. Its stone walls, narrow streets, nocturnal courtyards, cellars big as whales' bellies, were a thousand years old. The Danes had set up trading posts there. The Normans had walled the town. Protestants from planted lands had come and settled there. A shipload of Huguenots, fleeing from France with their fine craftmanship and chaste women, sought and found refuge there. During the Great Famine and the lesser famines the starving Irish had made their way up to its workhouse, where they died at the locked entrance gates.

It had survived because of its doubtful allegiance. Foreign armies had sailed into the harbour and red-faced Irish recruits had sailed out to charge in light and heavy brigades across the battlefields of France, Spain, Germany and southern Russia.

Above the municipality and close to the abattoirs stood a mountain of offal. On a warm day an audible cloud of midges about the mound could be heard far out to sea. Within this mountain of livers, guts, intestines and colons lived a colony of rats, the largest in the world. There was one rat, the father of them all, called Olc Mór, who appeared infrequently. He looked down on the town like a gargoyle on a cathedral spout. Sailors, hearing of this strange and fabulous rat, often visited the perimeter of the offal heap to catch a view of Olc Mór. It was beside the huge dam which turned the millwheels of the town.

Before the municipal fathers imported Chinese, to work in the factories and mills, they thought that they had a ready workforce on the island of Inis Orga. They had sailed to the island and there painted a bright picture of prosperity for the men who sat on the quayside walls smoking their pipes.

——We would be slaves to time instead of its master, the fabricators were told.

They offered two-storeyed houses but were told ——We could not live on top of one another. It's unnatural.

They offered large sums but the islanders said that they had little time for money and most of them preferred to compose poetry.

The military barracks of Baile was of eastern design. Minarets rose from its corners instead of towers. Long verandas opened to the thin sun of summer and the rheumatic winds of winter. In India, it was reported, there stood a granite military barracks. It was stiff and austere, a cube, standing four-square against the gales of the Atlantic, the snows of winter and the sallies of Irish rebels from bog and mountain slope.

There was great need for soldiery in Baile. There was constant fear that Murtagh McMurtagh would some day attack the town. He was served by the poet Raftery who carried songs in his head which inflamed the peasantry into rebellion.

The insane of Baile and the Barony of Skattery were housed in the asylum, grim-walled, grey-walled and outer-walled. The insane saw the morning or the evening light vicariously. They did, however, see the midday sun through iron bars. Beside the asylum stood the workhouse, equally grim but with no bars upon the windows.

Baile too had its fashionable streets and squares where the fabricators and merchants lived. It also boasted of a town hall where the councillors handed down council and judgement of doubtful value; here also the courts were held and the death sentence often passed on stray rebels from the Barony of Skattery.

Beneath Baile lay a forgotten purgatorial world, as twisted as a labyrinth, with dark passages leading into and out of the catacombs. Lupus Ryan was king in the Catacomb of Saint Ita where the blind and the maimed lived. With a bright eye and a blind one he looked out upon his kingdom. He was a wise ruler. The day had a slow ritual measured by the various bells. He preserved decorum among the inmates, which tempered their despair.

Albus Crow was the present ruler of the Catacomb of Saint Jude. Here the lepers lay on straw, the white disease eating their flesh silently, like shapeless sea monsters. When a member of Saint Jude's died his body was thrown into a stream, which ran beneath, and was carried out to the harbour. Here they listened only to the beating of their own hearts. They spoke rarely. No king ruled here for long. Sometimes the throne was empty.

There was also the Catacomb of Saint Claude, reserved for the condemned. They were chained to the wall while they waited for the hangman to erect a ceremonial scaffold in Baile Square. Their despair was total. If they had to wait too long for execution they went mad. They lived outside the borders of charity.

In the middle distance and mostly at night, Noah McNulty built his salvific ark. It was constructed from the carcasses of old ships, discarded planks and timber oddments. Upon the day of the deluge it would carry him southwards.

Thus Baile was complete in every way. It was well-defended by walls and a military barracks. It was a tolerant place to live in, as could be observed from the many creeds which worshipped their own strange gods there. It was a prosperous town: the public coffers were filled with gold. It was a sane place: the insane were locked away. It had lasted for a thousand years. It would survive another thousand.

Anna Morphy arrived in Baile. She took rooms at the Imperial Inn. Each morning she ordered a coach to be brought to the courtyard. Dressed in silk, her face hidden by a pious veil, she drove through the town to the local churches. Her talk on these occasions was interspersed with French phrases, like red plums in a cake. Her gestures were Parisian and fine. It was known that Madame Morphy was a widow. It was said that she had returned from France where she buried her husband, a famous French marshal. She gave alms to the poor and made a donation of gold sovereigns to the Large Sisters of Saint Ita.

When she observed Berwick Square it reminded her of tranquil squares in Paris and she knew that this one was most suited to her purpose. The reticent facade of Berwick House carried a well-bred disdain for the others in the square, which she liked.

She discovered that the possessor of this house was an old lady called Cecily Gorewood. She was ailing, eccentric in the best British fashion and lived with one hundred cats. Anna Morphy suddenly took an interest in cats.

—I am afraid I left mes chats in France, she told the innkeeper. I feel triste without them. I wonder if I could purchase some in Baile.

——The best one to consult on all these matters is Rapparee
Walsh. If there are cats in Baile he will find them. But beware
of his tricks. He'll sell you a tom-cat and swear that it has
taken a vow of chastity.

——How do you know?

——Well, Miss Gorewood takes in every stray female cat
which wanders the backyards of Baile. The bold Rapparee
became her cat collector. He ran out of stray ones so, one
night, raving drunk, he raided the convent and stole the
Reverend Mother's cat and brought it to Berwick House.
'He's a tom-cat, Miss Gorewood, but an exceptional one,'
Rapparee told her. 'I got him as a gift from the Reverend
Mother and he has taken a vow of chastity.' 'It's a grand
thing to know that there is virtue in the animal world,' she
replied. The Rapparee knew that if he continued his talk he
might make a few more shillings from the virtuous cat, so he
said, 'They think that he can see the spirits of the dead.
Every time he passes the statue of Saint Joseph in the cloister
he bows his head out of respect.' 'And why did the Reverend
Mother wish to get rid of him?' 'Because of Rodrigues who
states in his book that many sisters leave all their possessions
only to set their affections upon the convent cat. One night
the Reverend Mother was examining her conscience under a
glass window which represents the Holy Ghost and He talked
directly to her. He said, "Give the cat to Miss Gorewood."
So the cat comes with a reference from the Holy Ghost.' It
was soon apparent that the cat never had taken a vow of vir-
ginity. Miss Cecily Gorewood took Rapparee to court. The
solicitor, Saggitarium O'Connor, proved that Rapparee was
the offended party, that he had been induced to steal cats
and that Miss Cecily Gorewood was the recipient of stolen
goods.

——Have Rapparee Walsh sent to me, Anna directed.

Rapparee was aware of his green faded coat, his punctured
shoes, his unkept beard. Crumpling his hat in his hand he
knocked at her door.

——Entrez, she ordered, and pour yourself a drink.

He entered, bowed and poured himself a drink with a
half-forgotten elegance.

——I believe you know where one can acquire cats, she
said directly.

——Don't talk to me about cats. My dreams are disturbed
by cats, pawing around inside my head and tearing the back
of my eyeballs trying to get out.

He sipped the wine. It had a deep body, a bouquet which was rare in Baile, a colour full of scarlet pleasure. He held the glass to the light and looked into its charged heart. He forgot his faded raiment.

—Rich and rare and, if my palate does not deceive me, the wine is from the south-west of France, perhaps from a chateau overlooking the Gironne?

—The subject is cats, not wine. Here's a purse of twenty sovereigns. Fetch me twenty cats.

—No man ever turned from gold, he said, turning from wine. I am at your command, madame. Ce que femme veut, Dieu le veut.

—How long do you think this Gore woman will live?

—Six months, madame.

—Is she sane?

—Who is.

—No philosophy.

—She is scattered and credulous. She thinks that cats have eternal souls. I bury them in her cat cemetery and I recite some Latin verse and give an eulogy. I am the most reliable feline undertaker in town. She has a marble slab erected over each one, giving its name and particular virtues. They lie in small oak coffins. You will find her in her cemetery each day at noon.

—You are acquainted with all that is going on in Baile, Rapparee?

—It is my business, madame. It is my business.

—I need a coachman and valet. Would you accept the position?

—My raiment is soiled, as you can see.

—Find a coat of green velvet, black shiny shoes, breeches of brown corduroy and a coachman's hat. Bring me the bill.

—That I will, madame. I am now your faithful servant! I shall hold your confidence, mam. La parole est d'argent, le silence est d'or.

—Good. She dismissed him with a delicate gesture of her plump hand.

He went in search of cats and the accoutrements of a coachman. His stars, so long at variance, were now agreeable to themselves.

The next day, as twelve rang out from the various steeples, the coach carrying Anna Morphy and driven by Rapparee Walsh stopped in front of the small, sequestered cat grave-yard. She pushed aside the iron-wrought gate and walked across the weedless gravel to where the cats lay buried in mathematical order. Cecily Gorewood entered. After some moments of silent contemplation the women drew near to each other and conversed for a long time. Anna Morphy told of her French cats and described their royal pedigree and their habits: one cat had belonged to the House of Orleans.

——I wonder what shall happen the cats when I pass over? It is a matter which causes me great anguish, Cecily Gorewood said.

——Many cats will be waiting for you on the far side.

——I know, and I look forward to the day. I believe the rivers there carry creamy milk down to a white sea.

——So I have heard.

——But what of my cats here? I wonder if I would be remiss in asking you to take care of them. I could leave the house in your name and put aside an annual sum towards the upkeep of the house and cats, for I am indeed a wealthy woman. My dear Anna, you have a large heart and there is room there for my cats. I shall sign all the necessary documents as I have many cousins who would claim my wealth when I die.

——Knowing how heartless cousins can be towards cats, I will accept your offer.

——You are a kind woman, Anna.

Anna Morphy departed. She called Rapparee Walsh.

——I wish to meet Saggitarium O'Connor.

——Very well, madame, I shall arrange the meeting.

That night, when Venus was in conjunction with Mars, she mounted the stairs to the solicitor's tower where he observed the stars. Beneath, Walsh waited patiently in soft velvet, buckled shoes and corduroy breeches. All night Venus was in conjunction with Mars. As dawn broke Anna Morphy came down from the tower, tousled and tired, a legal document in her hand. Rapparee Walsh kept his own counsel.

Next day Cecily Gorewood signed the conveyance and was impressed by the rider at the end which stated that with her money the house would be refurbished and certain ladies invited to reside whose duty it would be to take care of cats.

It remained for Cecily Gorewood to die, which she did calling out the names of long-departed cats whom she was now to follow into a doubtful eternity.

Anna Morphy took possession of the house. Many of the cats died. Ten survived; they were necessary if she were to remain within the legal limits of the will.

She restored the house to its original splendour. Within, the rooms were refurbished. She had a Persian Room, an Indian Room, a room which resembled the Alhambra and a Byzantine Room which was designed and executed by Noah McNulty, now short of ark capital. And when he had finished this room he set about installing gas lights. It was because of these red gas lights that the municipal councillors of Baile rented one of the largest rooms in Berwick House for periodic deliberations.

Humper O'Donaghue had been quarried out of the womb in the townland of Kish, about ten miles from the town and deep in the mountains. He was fifteen pounds when he was born, broad as he was long, big-headed, back-twisted and ugly. His cries were the cries of a black goat.

——He could have been fathered by Satan, the midwife said as she looked at him. One of his feet is clubbed.

She carried him to his mother's pap but he refused the nipple.

——He'll die for the want of nourishment, his mother said. Every natural child takes to the pap when he is put to it.

——He is the spitting image of you, the nurse told her.

——He's not. He's not. Throw him from the cliffs into the sea and let the waves have him.

——There is many an ugly infant turned into a handsome man.

——What doctor can straighten his back? And what shoemaker can make a pair of shoes for him?

——Now we must take what comes, the good and the bad, who knows but he might be a genius of some sort.

He would have died for the want of mother's milk but he dragged himself to the pig sty, trampled a litter of bonhams to death and usurped their aliment.

——Any child who suckles an animal, the midwife said, minting an idiom, but takes part of the quality of the animal into its blood.

He thrived on sow lactage: at eight his chest was barrel-wide, his head as big as an Aberdeen turnip, his legs firm as standing stones; his appetite was as large as the bill of a pelican and as wide as a cauldron; his thirst well-deep and early in life he had also acquired a taste for black porter, which he drank by the bucket.

——I don't know what I'll do with him at all, his mother often complained. He never talks. He eats more than a regiment and he'd drink a wake-house dry. He'll drive us to the workhouse. We might as well jump and become Protestants to keep him in soup.

The rumour that the Donaghues were thinking of joining the foreign religion became fact when it reached the mouth of the valley. A letter was sent to the Bishop. He called his synod. They considered the problem from every angle both acute and obtuse and decided to set aside a stipend for him. With this he would be both fed and clothed. Also an acre of church land was allocated to grow potatoes to feed him.

But Humper Donaghue could pay his own way: his strength was in proportion to his appetite. He had the power of a *meitheal* of men. He needed no sleep, except when the moon was in eclipse and during that dubious time he fell asleep for a month, like the northern bear. At twelve he was doing the work of ten normal men; at fourteen, eighteen; at sixteen, twenty-five. He could sow a field of potatoes in a day, sickle ten acres of wheat, flail a barn of oats and mix twenty troughfuls of pig mash. His sustenance during these high periods of activity was a cauldron of potatoes, twenty heads of cabbage, forty turnips and three sides of bacon. He was hired out to farmers by his mother, who became a rich woman. He worked alone in the fields, unable to tolerate the presence of other men.

It was Anna Morphy who first thought of bringing Humper Donaghue to Baile.

——One could make money out of horse dung, she told the councillors who had gathered into one of the large rooms of Berwick House.

——Why do you say so?

——Well, where there's muck there's money, and I say there is money in Baile.

——Make it, Anna, they said. For Baile is a filthy place. We will give you two acres of municipal land as a dung depot.

——And if I fail?

——Then we shall have free access to the Persian Room at any time of the day or night.

——Done. And she paid a visit to Saggitarium O'Connor who drew up the legal agreement.

——I can't see the future of horse dung, he told her.

——There is if it is gathered into one place. I'll concentrate all the horse dung of Baile.

——And what will you do then?

——I'll ship it to Africa and Egypt, where it is most needed, in the new ship I bought, *The Saint Fursey*.

——There is no knowing what goes on in your head, Anna.

Anna could not say when she first heard of Humper Donaghue. It could have been from a Greek sea captain or Rubini, the Italian Grandee. She had a part for Humper Donaghue to play in her grand scheme.

One day she ordered her carriage. Accompanied by Rapparee Walsh, and a bag of gold, she set out across the mountains and drove into the valley of Kish. It was fallow and famished. Beneath the shadows of Silurian and Ordovician mountains she discovered the wonder and the mother of the wonder.

——He's an infliction. There is no mother in Ireland ever dropped a son like him, she said in bad reference.

——Perhaps I have a job for him if he's intelligent, Anna told her.

——Is there money in it for his poor mother?

——There is.

——Well, I'll send for him then.

He was sent for and came. He wore size eighteen boots which were dripping with cow dung ooze and his nose carried a stalactite of snot.

——There is a great woman from the city to see you, his mother told him when he entered the house.

——And there was a captain from China yesterday, and a circus owner the day before, and an evolutionist the week before last, he complained.

——Tell me this, Anna Morphy asked directly, do you know how to heap manure?

——What class of dung had you in mind?

——Horse dung.

——That's hard. It is chained and falls apart. How high do you wish to heap it?

——House high, maybe higher.

He scratched the hard stubble on his chin and said ——For that you would need length and breadth.

——I have two acres of ground.

——Well, given a space like that you could hump it tower high, but you would have to layer it with straw. I could do it if I had a barrow broad enough, a spade big enough and a twelve-pronged fork.

——I could have all these made for you by the Huguenots
at the Isle of Geese, but first you must pass three tests. Did
you ever hear of Puchán Bachach, the goat?

——Yes. He's the father of all goats. He lives on Salachar
Mountain, the one that has gored nine men and is bigger than
an ass.

——That's the goat, yes. Well, I want his head and horns.
The pelt you can keep for yourself.

He left the kitchen and set out upon his first test. With
him he took his reaping hook and food for four days. He
tracked the goat through the wilderness, following his pebbly
droppings on the trampled ferns. He discovered him in congress at the end of a valley, close to the skeletons of several
men.

The great goat looked at him with hot eyes. The two
faced each other, cautious of guile. The Puchán Bachach bent
his head and charged with scimitar horns. Humper threw himself aside from the menacing prongs. The Puchán Bachach,
anticipating this, turned with him and plunged his horns into
the dwarf's chest. Spitted, he was dashed by the Puchán
against the granite face of a large boulder. Humper, sum-
moning his strength, prized himself from the horns and
twisted onto the goat's back like a Minoan bull-acrobat. He
grasped the horns firmly. Over mountain and hill the Puchán
Bachach ran, struggling to free himself from the dwarf who
had his clubbed foot planted deep in his belly. Humper was
master. He guffawed at the stars and heaped desecration on
the moon. When the old progenitor was tired Donaghue took
his sickle from his belt and severed the head from the body.
He tore off the hide and later cured it in sea-weed. He made
it into a vest which in time grafted itself to his flesh and he
became part-goat.

——There you are, mam, he said when Anna Morphy
opened the door of Berwick House. I have the head and the
horns in a bag.

——Come up stairs and into my room, she invited. I have
a barrel of red wine for you. You deserve a warrior's prize.

He drank the wine and received a warrior's prize until
dawn broke in the eastern sky.

——And now, you must go and pluck the feathers from the
Black Ravens of Slasta.

The ravens rooked in primal yews about the old manse of
Slasta. They ate the flesh of beggar and sheep and fed off the

mountain of offal. It was said that they were the souls of old, damned women who had held truck with hell during their lives.

Humper Donaghue sat at the bone mill and studied them when they came like a plague at evening time, sweeping through the clouds of midges which buzzed about the offal heap and carrying away tangled ropes of gut.

He climbed the hill of offal and gathered fresh guts. He wrapped them about his body and padded the meshes with pancreas and liver and gizzard. Then he went and stood beneath the yews of Slasta. The trees were raucous with noise. The birds swooped down upon Humper Donaghue. As they did he cut at them with his sickle. For three days they waged war upon him and then they were defeated. He plucked the dead ravens, stuffed their feathers into huge bags and carried them to Anna Morphy.

She gave Humper two barrels of wine and bound his raven wounds. He lay on raven feathers and received a warrior's reward.

—What's next? he asked when dawn was filling the eastern sky.

—Did you ever hear of the Viper of Mucker? I want the skin from his back.

With a bag of quicklime upon his back and a pronged fork in his hand he set out.

He walked far into the mountains before he discovered the den of the Viper of Mucker. Coiled about five bullocks, it looked down on him. There were ten eyes in its observant head. Sensing prey, it uncoiled and fastened itself about Humper Donaghue. It carried him upwards. Freeing his arms, he poured the quicklime over its eyes and cauterized vision. Holding the pitchfork above its tortured head, now blind and confused, he thrust the prongs deep into the cupola of brain. Green slime spurted up about the prongs and ran down its coils. The long body twitched. Humper Donaghue tore the living, iridescent skin from its back. He left the viper to putrify and made his way back to Baile.

He presented Anna Morphy with the flayed hide, drank three barrels of wine and after his Herculean task fell asleep, unable to reap a warrior's reward.

Later during the week he began his work as horse dung collector and cairn builder of Baile. He had a broad barrow, a wide shovel and a twelve-pronged fork. Each morning, as the cocks crowed behind netted wire and proclaimed the

doubtful presence of the dawn, he left the yard in search of
dung. His journey took him through the tangle of streets
under arches, between gate posts of stone, over cobbles and
into dim interiors.

He soon began to judge men by the quality of their horse
dung. For the small farmer he had little regard. His horse
was so ill fed that it yielded only small piles of dried manure.
Those of the merchants yielded a better grade but not lavish.
The horses of the rakes, stabled beside Berwick Square, were
animals fit to carry gods. Well fed, well groomed, practiced
at the hunt and the steeplechase, they gave double yield like
a good field.

And all the dung he carried back to the Spanish Yard. He
began by building it six inches high and spread it over an acre.
He layered it with straw to bind the fragile texture together.
When the heap was door-high he would reduce the layer to
four inches. Later he would alternate an inch of dung with an
inch of straw.

He did not discover all the secrets of cairn building immediately. His first heap collapsed when it was roof high. It flowed
down the streets and out into the sea. The people protested.
Then the councillors objected. They donned their ermine
and chains and brought Humper into their oaken council
chamber. Failure had drained his strength. For the moment
his mind, like his cairn of dung, had collapsed.

——Concentrate your dung and don't have it running
through the town. It has stained everything.

——I will, my lords. I will. He whinged on bended knee.

——How high do you expect to build it?

——Given a chance, my lords, Town Hall-high.

——No one ever built a cairn of dung Town Hall-high, they
roared down at him. And do not use burough images when
you refer to horse dung.

——It is only a way of putting it, my lords. When a man
builds he can only use the proportions of things standing
about him for comparison.

——That's a fair answer, they mumbled to one another,
bowing up and down with semi-wise heads. How can you
hope to build it Town Hall-high?

——Stakes will stabilize it, my lords, I'll beat them into
the ground and root the dung in the earth.

They were satisfied with their inquisition. Humper returned
to the Spanish Yard. Now his days were long and balanced.
His task was an endless one, like the rotation of the planets.

He detested, however, the twists in the streets, the bad entrances to back yards, the small returns for long journeys. Towns were badly planned, he often thought to himself. Cormac McMurtagh, who had tried to bring him on to the Revolutionary Committee, had the right idea about town planning. He said that all roads should be straight and houses standard.

He built and finished his first cairn of dung in three months. It rose roof-high and was visited by many strangers. It was ready for *The Saint Fursey* when she cast anchor in the harbour. He spent a month filling the hold of the ship. Then she weighed anchor and set sail for Oriental ports. Humper was left with a green memory and an empty yard. His labours began again. Ambition grew in his mind. He would build a cairn bigger than a town hall. When he had unlocked the secrets of architecture he would put a steeple on it.

Thoughts grew within Humper Donaghue's head, and moved like grey tangled eels. They turned and twisted and burrowed within his skull.

——I will raise a monument to myself if it lasts only a day, he told himself. I will shape the horse manure into something which placates my eye, or die from the tedium of pushing horse turds through twisted streets which cut off the light.

There was no definite day or hour when he decided to build an edifice more spacious than the Linen Hall or raise a tower higher than that of the Baile steeples. Passing through the town, he would put down his barrow before the facade of the Linen Hall and gather in its proportion and balance. At night he stood beneath the steeples and wondered at their majesty. They displaced the stars, and very few men had displaced the stars or stretched out to pluck them from the branches of the night.

——I will ornament my building with serpents, goats and ravens. It might not last forever, but if it stands for a day or a week it will be remembered forever. And it would need a bell to give it finish. I will cast the largest bell ever cast and it will rage against all others.

So he gathered brass cannon and buried them in a cairn of dung and continued to build.

The inhabitants of the municipal town of Baile looked at the building rising from above the houses. It was dark and green like the thoughts of the devil.

He roofed it with thatch and began to construct the tower.

When it was finished four windows faced the cardinal points. He placed strong wooden beams in the tower. From the cross beams he would hang his bell.

He went into Mucker Glen, where he had killed the viper, and prepared to cast the bell. Ten times he tried but each time the mould collapsed. By error he learned the art. He built a huge furnace to melt the cannon guns. He fashioned a clay mould into a bell shape. He coated it thick with bee's wax. Over this he put an outer moulding of clay. He boiled the wax and drew it away and poured liquid bronze into the mould. He then let it harden for a fortnight. When he broke away the clay he discovered a bell larger than himself. It was larger than any bell in Baile. For the moment he would leave it tongue-dumb. Then, on a stormy night when the winds were wild, it would beat out brazenly across the rooftops.

Under the cloak of darkness he went into the Glen, loaded the bell on to the barrow and brought it across uneven roads to Baile. It was knocked this way and that. When he reached the Square he discovered that it was cracked.

—A curse on it! It will have a raucous voice and peal no charm.

After he had hung the cracked bell he had a congressional meeting with Anna Morphy in her Byzantine Room. To reach this room he went down into the Burrows of Baile and followed winding passages until he reached the trap-door.

—What's this I hear about the cairn of dung? she asked, later. They say it will rise taller than any building in town and as high as a religious steeple. You could be driven outside the bounds of the church for presumption.

—I am already.

—You are a black one and the world within your head Stygian. Do you believe that life is the end of all?

—Life is something I endure like a sickness. The dead are dead and their bones have no cohesion. Their flesh has melted, their sinews and their muscles untuned. Bones hold firmness for a while, but then they become powder.

—You talk like a preacher.

—Flesh is like butter. This town too will fail.

—But it is built to last forever.

—Time will sandpaper it down, if Noah McNulty's famous deluge does not sweep it away.

—His world is not dark and constricted like yours. Look at the ceiling he painted for me. So well did he paint it that it looks like a dome in a great cathedral.

They looked at the dome of golds and blues, and Byzantine rectitude. From some Eastern sky bright light poured in the painted windows.

——That is the world to which his ark will take him, she said.

——He's already there. For him there is no dark side to anything. Time and sun does not blister him as it does me.

——There is a black bias in your mind. Where do you get your rhythms and feelings?

——From the Shakespearean actors that came to Baile and played to small audiences. I crouched in the circular window and listened to them.

During the congressional night they talked of many things. The Morning Star was barely visible when he let himself down into the trap-door under the bed and made his way through the Burrows.

The Burrows branched in many ways, illogically. The narrow tunnels of weeping slabs were built a long time ago. Summer here came through small street grills. It was a world of shadows. Humper Donaghue knew those who lived in this strange world of thin, rationed light.

He entered the Catacomb of Saint Ita, ruled by Lupus Ryan. When they heard his approach they dragged themselves across the straw floor on stumps of legs, or fingered the walls which led to the tunnel opening.

——What were her eyes like? asked the blind.

——They are like the sun, he told them.

——And what room were you in?

——The room of Byzantium, with its golds and its blues and its heavenly lights. It is an imagined heaven.

——How does one go to this heaven?

——By all accounts, in the boat which Noah McNulty builds.

——And her eyes in passion?

——Bright as the portholes of hell. Even brighter.

——And are her limbs perfectly shaped? the deformed asked.

——Yes. One leg is as long as the other and she walks without a limp. There is no hump upon her back and she has all her fingers. Her face is as balanced as it should be, with two eyes above the nose, red lips about her mouth and her full compliment of teeth.

They always asked the same questions and he always gave the same answers. When he was finished he went down through the passages and into the Catacomb of Saint Jude where the lepers lay supporating.

—What was her flesh like? they asked.

—Wholesome as bread.

—Had it any blemish, black spot, deep pock-mark or heavy blue veins?

—It had none of these things. It was like untrampled snow.

—And what of its scent?

—It fills the nostrils with perfume, as if you were walking in the Queen's garden upon a summer's day.

—Do you think that her flesh will corrupt with age?

—Doesn't every woman's flesh. Was there ever a fine woman born who did not wither and wrinkle in the end?

—No.

—Well, she is subject to the same harsh laws. And some day she will be as dry and brittle as barn hay.

Humper then questioned them about the living and the half-dead.

—No one died today. Cloynes, there, might be dead tomorrow. He hasn't uttered a word in a week. His heart is softening, they told him.

—I'd better bring a sack the next time I'm coming. Did he say where he wished to be buried?

—No. It's equal to him. He has relations in America, but he hasn't heard from them for years.

—Well, I'll put him away safely in Lord Dingle's crypt and it hasn't been used for a dozen years. I have the key.

—If we hadn't you to take care of us, we would be badly used.

—Don't worry about your final resting place. I have the leaden coffins open and ready for you. I have thrown out the first and the third Lord Dingle. There was little left of them, other than a normal man's bones and a few rings upon their fingers.

—It is grand to know that we will end our days in the company of the nobility.

After he had given them consolation he continued down along the passages, kicking rats out of his way. They were a low, graveyard breed with thin bellies, mangey coats and sharp white teeth. They bore no relationship to the rats of Sliabh Feola.

The final room was the prison dungeon, reserved for the condemned. They sat chained to the wall, their eyes glazed with gibbet fear. They could hear the hangman hammering nails into the platform of the scaffold.

——Did you see him making it? they asked.

——Yes.

——Is it in the middle of the square or at the corner?

——In the middle.

——He must expect a large audience. When he expects a poor audience he builds it in the corner. Do you think the ladies will come in their fine carriages?

——They will. They want to see Frank Fallon swing, the one that killed the parish priest with the blackthorn stick. Is there a Frank Fallon here?

——There is, over in the corner, raving since they chained him to the wall.

——And what's he raving about?

——All sorts of things. He's been calling for last year's snows. He calls, too, for his shrunk old mother, who prays to the saints in the stain-glass windows. He must have been in a seminary.

——It is always hard when intelligent men have to face the gallows. The black pit holds terror for them.

Frank Fallon looked at Humper Donaghue and said ——All the fine flesh will be eaten by the birds and my bones will be crushed to ashes. This body is anointed like the anointed one I killed. It will hang from the gibbet, the rains of heaven washing it, the sun scorching it black. It's a terrible thing to be gibbet-hung and at the whim of the wind, now blown east, now blown west. I have no wish to die.

Humper Donaghue sat beside Frank Fallon. He could see in the quarter-light his fine, dissolute face. It was red and patched with dissipation.

——Why do you wish to live, more than the others?

——Because I know the taste of the sweetness of life.

——It's a pity that such an intelligent mind should be quenched. The priest is dead and tomorrow another must die to equal the balance. The judge and the jury who condemned you are now eating from rich tables, certain of another day. It is a pity that you should die, that you should not see next year's snows.

——It is indeed.

——How many times have you died today?

——Oh, at least ten times.

——Well, that's enough. There is no reason why you should die again. Who is master of the law and who can pass fair judgment upon any man?

With that final thought he bit off the pins which held the manacles in place about the prisoner's hands and said —Follow me now, before the jailers discover that you are free. He pushed open the huge wooden door, they raced along the corridor, up the stairs and into the small room where Humper Donaghue lived.

—I'll leave the dust of this town behind me. I shall now wait for the snows of winter with joy, declared Fallon as he bid good-bye to his rescuer.

The fugitive passed across the square. The gibbet stood above him. Ten times that day he had been hanged upon it. He looked at it for a moment and then he disappeared down a medieval alley-way.

Humper Donaghue sat at a deal table after Frank Fallon had left. His mind was gloomy as he ate oatmeal bread and drank sticky, black porter. Later he went to a barrel of salted pigs' feet he had stolen from the quays, took out ten feet and tore the flesh and gristle.

—I'll finish the tower, he told himself. And I'll hang the bell. It will be tongued with a cannonball. The wind will carry its cracked voice out over the city, into the mountains and on to the sea.

His thoughts were disturbed by the rapping of emaciated knuckles at the door.

—Who's that, this hour of the morning?

—It's me. The Wandering Spanish Friar, now Cardinal Pachomius.

—Where did you come from?

—From the ark, where Noah McNulty poured oil upon me.

—Well, keep going. I'll have no truck with cardinals.

—If you don't open the door, I'll let the town know how you cast a bell from stolen British cannon and buried it in a manure heap.

—How do you know that?

—There are lots of things which I know and others don't. There is a voice in my head which tells me many things.

—Are you a regular cardinal?

—No, a wandering one. I wander from place to place, reading from small, pious books.

—I'll let you in. He opened the door. —You are very thin.

—I know. I eat berries when they are in season, I catch trout in streams, and when I am by the sea I prize barnacles from the rocks.

——Why this thin diet?

——It kills temptation.

——When had you temptation last?

——Twenty years ago.

——Sit by the fire.

——I never sit by the fire. That brings on temptation. I keep my blood cold.

——That is a strange type of cloak you wear, not at all like a cardinal's.

——I know. It's my habit. I made it from pieces of cloth I picked up travelling around the world. The hood is made from the shirt of Judas. I bought it from a relation of his in Jerusalem. The main part is made from the sail of Saint Peter's boat and my trousers are from the shroud of Lazarus. The shoes are from the hide of one of the sheep herded by Saint Patrick. My cord is made from Nile reeds plucked directly from the spot where Pharaoh's daughter discovered Moses floating in the basket.

——You must be a holy man, surrounded by so many relics.

——I am.

The Wandering Spanish Friar sat in the shadows, away from the fire. His face was phosphorescent. It lent a little light to the dim corner.

Humper ravaged a pig's foot.

——Do you want a chew? he asked. ——No, I only eat fish. He tossed the central bone into the fire. He drank some porter. ——Do you want a drop of porter? ——No, I only drink water. ——What brought you here? ——The smell of sin. ——What does it smell like? ——It smells of a thousand things, porter, fine linen, street dust, gold, and Continental music. ——Music has no smell. ——It has. I got the same smell once in Corinth. ——What do you finally believe? ——That the town will be destroyed. ——So does Noah McNulty. But he will float away in his ark on the day of the deluge. ——No, he won't. It will be destroyed by fire and not by water. ——And what will happen my noble building? ——Forked lightning will lodge in it and it will be burned. You will burn with it. ——Who told you all this? ——The voice inside my head. ——Well now, a voice outside your head is telling you to ship yourself out of here. I'm tired of lamentations.

He caught the spectral figure and threw him on to the street. He returned to the fire. His mind was morose. Black images floated up from the bottom of his mind. He saw a bull, fin-backed; a fish with human legs; a serpent with a thousand arms, which took to the sky on bat wings. It became a green cloud and discharged poisonous rain. His eyes rolled and he fell on the floor, disgorging pig flesh and porter.

God was grey and hell was hot. So thought Noah McNulty the Ark Maker. He had been making the ark for six years and it would take him to Byzantium. To the councillors he was insane. To the few disciples who had been drawn to him, he was a prophet.

Byzantium was a jaded place, without passion, untroubled. It was a domed place, hierarchical, cool of colour, tranquil of image, an anchorite place ruled by archimandrites. It was far away beyond troubled seas, unbeaten by cold winds.

Noah worshipped a firm god, severe, harsh and well over a hundred, with sunken cheeks, furnace-bright eyes, a grey dignity of years. The picture of this Eastern god hung on the wall of his shoemaker's shop, eight feet tall, four feet wide. It had been carried from Constantinople by the Wandering Friar and purchased by Noah. It passed judgement on all who visited the shop, casting its sharp light on the dark corners of their souls.

—I'll set Noah McNulty's god after you, mothers said to troublesome children when all other measures failed. Noah's god stood guardian over the minds of all the children of Baile. They knew that he was looking into their souls, searching out their sins. If they offended he would bury them for eternity in the fires which burned at his feet.

—Look long and look well, Noah would say to the faithful few. And tell me what you see.

—A severe god with his head among the stars and his feet planted in scorching flames.

—And what is he saying?

—Repent, repent.

—And what else is he saying?

—Nothing else today.

—That's right. He has nothing else to say today. Tomorrow if you listen you will hear something different.

He spent his day cobbling shoes. He needed little to sustain him, a loaf of bread, dark cheese, a jug of milk. With the small profit he made from his long hours he bought planks of wood, nails, tar and paint. On a wall stood a rough picture of the ark. It was shaped like a large currach and when finished

it would be about fifty feet long and about twenty feet wide.
A tapering pine carried a rough sail, with spiral and lozenge
decorations. Above the sail stood a barrel-shaped crow's nest.

In the bulk of the ship lay the animal quarters. In these
pens he would place a pair of asses, horses, goats, a cock and
a hen, a goose and a gander, a cow and a bull. There was
also a space for seed potatoes, cabbage plants, turnips and
oats. In a further compartment, in a nine inch bed of clay,
he would put sally, oak, ash and beech saplings for the new
old earth of Byzantium. From the prow of the boat pro-
truded a gargoyle-shaped image, teeth bared to an imagined
sea.

In the yard behind the shop the half-finished boat rested.
The base was already completed but the upper part showed
bare ribs. The pine mast was in place and from it hung a
ragged sail, which has been catching backyard wind for four
years. In the paddock grazed the sets of animals which
would accompany the ship on its journey.

Noah was certain that the half-finished ark would bear up
under the deluge of water and carry him across the seas.

—And when will the flood come? he asked his faithful.

—Any day now. Any day now.

—And what will hapen?

—The heavens will split at the seams, like the day Tom
Duff's trousers split and him going up the ladder. Water will
pour down on the cursed town of Baile and wash away its
stones, its roofs and its houses of sin.

—And why do you believe all this?

—Because you said it, Noah.

He was never certain of the day of reckoning. But the day
would come, of this he was certain. There was no cloud of
doubt in his mind.

—Brothers and sisters, six years ago I saw the vision on
Knobber Hill. A cloud came down on me, and me drunk and
dissolute on my way home from the tavern. Brethern, I heard
a voice calling to me. It said, 'Noah McNulty, you cross-eyed
reprobate, give up your bad habits and kill your evil inclina-
tions. There is none worse than you for the women of
Skattery. You have indulged and stewed in the sweet wine
of white evil.'

—What answer did you give to the voice, Noah?

—I'll admit, I'll admit I cried. I'm the one who deflowered
the finest women in Connaught and got a widow-woman with
twins. I'll admit to it in a court of law. And I throttled a

man once in a post town and stole his money, and I passed
lead for silver.

——What was the voice like, Noah?

——It was the solemn voice of a man of a hundred-and-four.

——The god of the picture?

——The very same. It froze the blood in my veins and
brought all my transgressions before me, one by one and very
slowly. 'Wretch, McNulty,' it said. 'Hell isn't hot enough or
eternity long enough for you.'

——What did you say to that?

——'I'll promise anything,' I said.

——And what did he say after that?

——'Unflower yourself and remove the roots of concupiscence.' 'I will,' said I. 'And then build a boat.' 'I will. Give me
the plans.' 'Never mind the plans. Build a boat.' 'But I'm only
a shoemaker.' 'You are contrary, like all shoemakers. Can
you swim?' 'No.' 'Well, go and build a boat, for the deluge is
coming.' 'And when is the hour of doom?' 'Doom will come
in its own hour. Be prepared!'

There was always a doubt in Noah McNulty's mind, he did
not know whether the voice came from the inside or the outside of his head. He had heard voices before on the narrow
roads home from the tavern, when the trees became reprimand-
ing shapes, the wind took tongue, gaps in ditches bayed and
the moon yawned a fevered mouth. Better be sure. Better
follow the voice. Others had followed other voices.

Upon that night six years ago, his mind in ferment, he went
into his workshop and sharpened his shoemaker's knife. He
ran through the streets calling himself and all others to
repentance. The crowds gathered about him. He danced like
an Indian dervish, the world wheeled about him. Images
fermented. With a slash of his knife he killed *les fleurs du
mal*. Tortured of mind, he ran to the battlements of the
town and spiked them among the rotten gallow's heads. The
Ravens of Slasta, scenting unusual carrion, rose up from the
old trees, set up a commotion inside the right shield of the
moon and flew to Baile. *Les fleurs du mal* were carried
south and McNulty's mind, tranquil and untroubled, set out
for Byzantium.

He was carried to the military hospital. The dental-surgeon
poured a bottle of whiskey down his gullet and cauterized
with pitch the wounds on his groin. He survived, but the sap
of life had grown thin within him. He grew small. Thin bones

appeared under his cheeks. His skin rutted and turned ash colour. A patina of madness glistened in his eyes. His voice became senile. Now his oddnesses began to appear.

He started to collect religious books and statues. He had the works of all the mystics and a copy of the Koran. His collection of skulls, which he carried in a sack when he went from place to place, also dated from this time. In his workshop a skeleton, held together by hempen thread and secured to the rafters by a rope, dangled a foot above the floor. It swayed this way and that, following the directions of eccentric drafts.

Noah was not satisfied with his own doubtful conversion. He wished also to draw others into the vortex of his madness. He spoke to his audience of skulls, set about his feet in a semi-circle. Nose-holed, they listened, their earholes bunged with clay.

—I'll call out the truth from the roof-tops. I'll bang my accusations on doors. I will not let Baile perish.

The grimacing skulls listened.

—I'll start with the Large Sisters of Saint Vitas, he said.

What he said to them in front of their narrow gothic windows should have remained unsaid. He accused them of vile sins, of luxurious sins, of sins that were not sins at all but natural and pleasurable functions. This continued for six mornings until the Reverend Mother, the biggest sister of the Sisters of Saint Vitus, rushed from the gothic doorway of the convent and knocked him over the head with a chamber-pot.

He next turned his attention upon the Friars. He spoke of sloth and the sins of gluttony and many other transgressions against the Koran.

—Death will feed upon your fat backsides and your collops. It will chew your ribs and suck out the soft marrow of your eyeballs, and when it has done that, death the sickler will throw you in the bone-yard where the devils will grind your bones eternally to powder.

Patient men, and more patient than the Sisters of Saint Vitus, they put up with him for a fortnight. Then, one morning as he opened his mouth to chant out their deadly sins, they rushed from the monastery, bundled him up, and threw him into the cesspool.

As he broke surface for the second time, he called after the retreating habits:

—You've heard my words and rejected them. The day of reckoning will come, is coming, and your brown robes won't save you from the licking flames of the ovens of hell, warmer than the oven in Pete Lavelle's Bakery.

With his rakish past, his memory and his lack of compassion for the weakness of the flesh, he knew too much. So one day he stood before the council chamber of the municipal town of Baile.

——He won't turn on his friends, the councillors said, pressing red noses against the stain-glass windows.

His high-pitched voice carried far and clearly. He called out their names and he called out their sins. He named days and dates and offsprings.

——McGovern, the publican, here be thy transgressions. For those with eyes to see, let them see a young lad in Vintner Street carrying around McGovern's big head. He didn't lick that big head, or the red hair, off the stones.

On he went, calling out a litany of wrongs.

——He's turned queen's counsel on us. There is nothing worse than a reformed reprobate, they said, one to another. And when we recall the drunken nights we had in his company, and the songs and the vows of friendship, and the high jinks with low women.

They sat at the council table and took and gave counsel.

——We will have to buy his silence, one said.

——How? asked another.

——Isn't he building a raft or something in his back yard? someone asked.

——They say it will be an ark to sail to Byzantium. He heard a voice out at Knobber Hill which commanded him to build a boat.

——Well, why not ship him off to wherever the hell it is. We have exiled trouble-makers before.

——But Byzantium doesn't exist. I checked it in an atlas.

——Well, it's in his head anyhow.

——The worst place in the world for anywhere to be. Get him up from the street and we'll promise to subsidize that damn ark of his. The sooner it's finished and launched the safer we all shall be.

Noah McNulty was brought into the council chamber. The councillors were kneeling on the ground, hands joined and muttering to themselves.

——We must not disturb them until they are finished, the councillor told McNulty.

——We have seen the light, brothers, we have seen the light, brothers, they jibbered together.

—You've seen the light? Noah asked.

—Yes, Brother Noah McNulty.

—And you will make great sacrifices?

—Yes, Brother Noah McNulty.

—And you are prepared to wear concupiscence belts?

—Yes, they said. Then they reflected. What's a concupiscence belt?

He told them, he drew a belt for them.

—It costs a lot to have such belts made. And who will have the keys?

—Your wives will have the keys.

They held their tempers.

—Who will make them?

—Pakey Keane, Noah McNulty said.

The blacksmith came. He was querulous and wondered why he had been called. They explained their problem.

—What's in it for me? he asked.

—What do you mean, what's in it for you, a fair price for a good article.

—Well, now that I know what's going on, my knowledge is of more value than it was.

—Nobody thinks of anything but money these days, the councillors complained.

—That's right. Every concupiscence belt will cost ten gold sovereigns.

—That's outrageous. One can buy the rim of a carriage-wheel for a sovereign.

—Take it or leave it, that's the going price.

Finally they agreed. Sixty sovereigns were put in a small coffer and handed to him.

On Thursday night Pakey Keane made his way up the back stairs with a sack of concupiscence belts on his back. The councillors in their longjohns were waiting for him. They had to admit to each other that Pakey Keane was a good blacksmith: even the stuffing on the inside was comfortable and no hard iron cut at flesh.

—Boys, we're spancelled for life, they said to each other, attempting to turn the serious occasion into a jocose one.

Then the blacksmith was told to wait outside. The keys were handed to Noah McNulty, who in person would deliver them at each councillor's home. They passed a motion, before he left, thanking him for protecting them from their follies and their weakness. When he had gone they recalled Pakey Keane.

——Where are the keys? they asked. We want to get out of
these belts. ——That's the first I heard about keys. ——What
do you mean? ——I was paid for belts and not for keys.
They flew into a municipal rage. ——Anger will get you no-
where. ——Well, what will get us anywhere? ——Twenty
sovereigns each for keys, he said, his eyes as cold as iron.

In the interests of nature they gave over twenty sovereigns
each for keys to their privacy. They would have, there and
then, throttled Pakey Keane, but as he held a municipal secret
they took refuge in patience.

Next evening McNulty stood again outside the municipal
buildings, chanting out their sins.

——There will be no end to this. We cannot attack him
openly now, let him have his cant. Later, when it is dark,
we will visit his workshop, they said.

They arrived at his backyard at nine.

——God bless the work, they chorused.

——He has, Noah McNulty said bluntly.

——You have imposed a heavy penance upon us, they said
to the figure standing inside the skeleton of the ark like
Jonah in the whale's belly.

——What penance?

——You locked us into concupiscence belts.

——That's the first I knew about it.

——You do not remember your promise of silence then?

——No, I can't remember anything these days, my brain is
scattered for some reason or other.

Fury rose in their minds like a high wind on an inland lake.
They chased him from among the ribs of the ark. Humper
Donaghue was passing by, pushing his wide barrow of horse
dung in front of him. They took Noah McNulty and threw
him on top of the manure.

——It's a harsh world, Noah gurgled to himself. And it is
best left alone. For it is bent upon its own frenzy and will
not be distracted. I don't know why I don't grab a nag and
gallop out of the town, instead of building an ark to float
out. There must be easier ways to get to Byzantium.

CHAPTER THREE

The Barony of Slattery had doubtful borders. The cartographers were more certain of its centre than its rim. It carried a fixed border only on the west, where it fronted the Atlantic. The eastern edge was uncertain.

The land was dismal and hungry. Thin grass nourished famished cattle and an isolated imagination. The McMurtagh tribes and sub-tribes inhabited this land. No Roman standards had been planted here. Neither had the plowshare of the Normans turned the starved soil.

The McMurtaghs were proud of their blood. It was old, purple, Celtic. Their bastards, they said, had more standing among genealogists than the royalty of Europe. This belief they firmly held, as toes hold nails, and it was nurtured by Hackett the Harper and Piobán McPludaire the Reciter.

Murtagh McMurtagh was descended from Adam. There was definite proof in the annals. Piobán McPludaire could trace the long line back four thousand and ten years to the day when the first McMurtagh, Adam McMurtagh, was created.

The Castle of Slattery went up and up from a narrow base. Its slit windows were gunbarrel-wide and there was a small battlement about the slated roof. It stood at the doubtful end of a long bog. Hills and mountains brooded over it and Murtagh McMurtagh brooded within it all like a bilious pagan god.

About the castle stood the walled paddock, grass-bare, sodden. From it the mangey horses would carry the leaders into battle when the time was ripe.

——Murtagh is a slow man to make up his mind, his people said.

——He thinks a lot and turns barony affairs about in his

mind like buttermilk in a churn. But when he has made his decision, there will be no turning back.

He did turn things about in his mind. He sought the advice of his captains. They were old and unenthusiastic. They advised him to consider. It was difficult to grasp any question totally, they said. This advice suited Murtagh McMurtagh. To commit himself to the field, to face defined enemies might shatter any illusion he had of conquering Ireland and setting himself up in barbarian splendour on the Hill of Tara.

—We'll wait for Spanish wine and Spanish help before we march on Baile. Some night, when the town is asleep, we'll march through its open gates, scale the walls and establish the Brehon Law on the foreign plot.

He was six-foot-eight, the same height as Brian Ború, and half a century old. His hair fell in unwashed ropes down his back, his moustache curved out over his jowls and tapered in at his chest. He wore the heavy purple cloak of his ancestors. He ate in it, he drank in it, he lived in it, and the smell of it was on women. Slung out from two hairy lobes of chest was a large paunch, white, sunless, soft. It bounded ahead of him as he walked. This pondrous weight of flesh emasculated his desire to lead his troops into battle.

During the bad weather of mist and fog which obliterated the mountains and the bog he often heaved himself into his large oak throne, surrounded by his men, and fell into reverie. He imagined looking down from the hill of Tara on a hot summer's day, at fat cattle grazing in rich meadows, at the ancient games, at the peaceful crowds gathered from the four corners of Ireland with their tributes. He had built fine halls about him on Tara and there were banquets and feastings. The harp had been declared the national instrument. His soldiers stood about him in green tunics. His kingdom would last for a thousand years.

—We'll repel the foreigners, burn their castles and slaughter their whelps. We'll establish nunneries and convents and rebuild the old churches, he often told the clan chieftains when they gathered about his table.

—We will, we will! Let us see the enemies and we'll show them what we're made of.

—And we'll march on Baile and clean out the brood of foreigners who have settled there.

—We'll scatter them the way a hawk scatters sparrows.

—The blood of the race will be cleansed. It will be made as white as snow.

——We'll drink to that, Murtagh.

——Drink we will, boys. Drink we will.

This was the verbal ritual of the feasts given by Murtagh McMurtagh. Stirred by enthusiasm they rose from their oak stools half as old as time, and drank their poteen.

——No aid can be expected from Inis Orga, he told them.

——They are a red-rotten lot. Rhymers and wasters who spend half a day over a sheugh of potatoes, looking for a word to describe the heel of a woman or the hoarse music of a thrush.

——Men were born for battle, for the skirl of the war pipes and the tuck of drums. It's time to have the long songs again. Call upon Hackett the Harper and Piobán McPludaire. Let them remind us of the past. A lot of bent things happened in our history and there is a lot of straightening to be done.

——And you are the boy to do it, Murtagh. Maybe now is the hour of destiny.

——Not yet, men, not yet. We'll know the hour when we see it. There will be definite indications in the stars. We must wait for the royal ships from Spain with wine and men. Don't rush into things. Too many battles have been lost through haste.

Hackett the Harper was snoring by the kitchen fire, his beard entangled in the strings of his harp. He had waited for fifty years to harp the McMurtagh clans into battle. He was dressed in a long, white robe, like a shroud, which was spotted with brown dribble.

——Wake up, wake up! the servants called. McMurtagh wants you to harp for him, up in the hall.

——Has help come from Spain, has help come from Spain? he wheezed.

——No. McMurtagh wants the past recalled.

He was so venerable and had been still for so long that his bones had become chalky and brittle. They lifted him carefully, afraid that he might crumple, and carried him into the banquet hall.

——Sing for us, Murtagh called. ——What's that? ——Sing for us, you coot! ——About what? ——About the past, you fool!

Hackett disentangled his beard from the harp strings and tightened them. He looked at his instrument wherein the spurious history of his race had taken refuge. His fingers nibbled at the strings. The hall was silent. Fire flowed through his body. The portals of history were opened. The songs were sad and in the minor key and they spoke of battles long ago. His voice was as thin as the horses in the paddock, his eyes carried all the sadness of a thousand years.

The gathered tribes sat mute. The music was stirring communal images within them. What they imagined they imagined together, so mutual were their aspirations and grievances.

—He is unlocking the tombs of our ancestors. Do you see them? Murtagh asked, froth on his lips, the fever of lineage surging in his blood. Harp hard, Harper. Harp hard, Harper.

Hackett threw himself at the strings. His body palpitated with power. He tore images from the past, flaying the flesh from his fingers. Out through the gates of the harp marched Brian Ború on his way to the wide shore of Clontarf. He rode a white Napoleonic charger and his old, paternal face was parchment dry, his beard white with wisdom. The High King of Ireland marched past them but remained in the one place.

—Mark my image upon his face, Murtagh called.

—It's unmistakable. The resemblance is strong.

—Didn't I always say I was descended from Brian Ború. What more proof do we need. Doesn't Piobán McPludaire sing it in the genealogies.

They were back in the year 1014. It was a fine morning north of the Danish village of Dublin. Howth had a purple heather glow. Long ships with barbarian prows pastured on the green waves.

—It's an unequal fight, the McMurtaghs roared. There are twenty Danes for every Irishman.

—Don't interrupt the battle, Murtagh called. God is on the side of the Irish. We have strong representation in heaven.

As far as their communal eye could see, every ship in the world was anchored in the bay.

—They must stretch over to England, we don't stand a chance, was the general comment.

—Wait the outcome, Murtagh told them.

Down from the sand dunes of Clontarf rushed the Irish. They splashed through the shallow waves, eager to redden their swords with Danish blood. The sun stood still for two hours when it was to the disadvantage of the Danes.

—The Saints of Ireland have their shoulders to the rim of the sun, Murtagh said.

Evening came. Dew fell. The sea thickened with blood. Stamped sand attended the laundering waves. The dead stiffened. The wind stood mute. Inertia filled the battle-weary.

Within his tent Brian Ború prayed. He prayed as no monarch prayed at a medieval shrine. He called upon the saints of Ireland, particularly those of his relations, to declare their allegiance.

In their imagination the McMurtaghs were within the tent. The flap was thrown open and in crept Citric the Dane, his face ugly as a Japanese theatre mask. He drew his sword.

—Look out, Brian, they roared. The bastard, Citric, is behind you. Duck your head.

But he never ducked. Their warnings could not change the course of history. A Danish sword severed Brian Ború's Irish head. Even as it rolled across the floor it retained its dignity.

The Harper let the strings run fallow for half an hour. The McMurtaghs waked Brian Ború. After a decent interval of mourning Hackett was ordered to play again.

He now played nature music. Quietly he stole in upon the strings like a practised seducer. Soon they saw an Ireland which might have been, which still might be if Murtagh got up from his wide backside.

Soft water plashed over waterfalls like the rustle of silk on the body of a great lady. Meadows teamed with milk and honey. Cattle chewed a rich cud, up to their udders in grass. Cloister bells rang out over the land. A wild elk, sniffing the presence of a hunter, bounded across the brown mountains. Always there was the warm Mediterranean sun, ripening the fruit and magical berries on the boughs and bringing summer to fruition.

The barbaric hearts of the McMurtaghs softened. Tears welled up in their eyes and ran down their cheeks and they all cried —We have a great past and a grand land.

—The light of Europe, were we given half a chance. Taken all in all, nobody will look upon our likes again, Murtagh told them.

—Amen to that.

—But don't lose heart, boys, the day will come when Ireland will be ours.

—We have been chosen by heaven, they said.

Hackett the Harper now realised that their souls were at rest. He snapped the threads of vision as he sobbed —I couldn't take any more. I couldn't take any more. My bloody heart would burst. Wake me up when help comes from Spain.

—Bring in McPludaire, Murtagh ordered. And we'll see where we all came from.

The maid-servants went down to the dungeons under the castle to find Piobán. He detested the light and lived in total darkness, emerging only to chant out the genealogical tree. He was the family reciter, the family memory, a bardic poet, an annalist.

He had survived the hardships and rigours of a bardic training. Twelve years he had spent as an apprentice, learning his trade and memorizing names, and the names that names give rise to when they marry, couple and spawn.

Piobán knew that he had betrayed the bardic oath. In professional circles he was known as McPludaire the Liar.

Many years ago he had arrived at the Castle of Skattery, hungry, demented, as lonesome as a heron against a low sky. Ushered into the presence of Murtagh, the first question he was asked was: 'Could you trace me back to Adam?' 'It's difficult, very difficult to do a thing like that as Adam goes back a long way.' 'Well if you can't do it, out on your backside you go.' The spectre of hunger had risen before Piobán McPludaire: 'Give me a week to think about it.' When he felt warm food in his stomach and soft wine upon his tongue, he betrayed the oath. He did what no true bard would do: he invented remote McMurtagh sires and traced the line back to Adam. In bardic circles from then on he was known as a reprobate and schismatic.

He stumbled into the hall, thin, sunless, half-transparent. There was a high glaze on his eye.

—There is too much to remember, too much to remember and if I forget it, then it is lost forever. Leave me in darkness for the light blots out names.

—Begin, they said.

—In the year two thousand five hundred and eighty B.C. the world was created. Six days later Adam McMurtagh was created and he had two sons by his wife, Eve McMurtagh, called Cain McMurtagh and Abel McMurtagh.

And on and on he went in a drone, like a stuck reed in a bagpipe chanter. It took him four hours to recite what he had to say. When he had finished the small seeds which Adam had planted had grown trunks and branches. It fell out that Murtagh was related to the King of Persia, the Emperor of Egypt, the King of Spain, the King of France and many others, a man of royal ooze.

—I'm a straight descendant of Adam and related to the best blood in the world. I could be sitting on the throne of Egypt instead of on a hard oak chair in the Castle of Skattery.

——Can I go now?

——You can, and remember who feeds you.

——Indeed I will, son of Adam McMurtagh.

He left the assembly hall and tottered back to his dungeon. A mouse was waiting for him. He sat on a stool and told him all that had happened.

Murtagh, elated by lies, stood upon his oak throne.

——We'll take Baile when we get Spanish aid. We'll march with the men from Madrid down the old bog road, and we'll follow the edge of the lake to the main highway. Then we will capture all Ireland. You'll be all crowned kings because you stood behind me during the bad days. Tara will be the new capital of Ireland.

——And we'll crown you King of Ireland and you sitting on the stone of destiny.

——And I'll found an all-Irish kingdom, filled with comely maidens, which will last a thousand years, when help comes from Spain.

While they sat in the dark hall, torch lit, half-lit, horse hooves clattered across the cobble castle yard.

——A letter from Spain, the messenger called. It's for Murtagh McMurtagh.

——Hurray! the young McMurtagh bloods and blades yelled. Aid at last. It is time to call the troops together and march.

——Wait, advised Murtagh. We must read the contents. Proceed with caution in all things. We have to take counsel.

The messenger placed the foreign parchment in front of him. The unbroken seal carried the arms of the King of Spain. Beneath it two ribbons floated like a fish tail.

——It's daintily done out, Murtagh said weakly. It would be a pity to break it.

——Let us hear the news.

——You'll hear it all in good time.

——We'll hear it now, they said in anger.

——All right. All right. Bring me light and a Spanish scholar.

They gathered about the yellow parchment, splashed with a Spanish royal seal. Reverence for the great monarch of Iberia prevented Murtagh from tearing it open. This was the first reply he had received to the fifty letters he had sent to the Escorial. Taking his dagger, he gently slit open the letter. He unfolded it and studied the foreign calligraphy, the arms of the court of Spain, smelt the southern comfort and handed it to the scholar. He translated.

Dear Don Murtagho de Murtagho,
Greetings from Spain. We have received your correspondence and have felt a warmth at your solicitous inquiries after Our health. It has been poorly this year as has been the health of Our Queen.

We have tried to trace relationships with you in Our records but Our genealogists can find no blood link between Our Houses. We and Our Wife feel the poorer as a result. We can only trace Our forebears back to the year 892 B.C. Before this Our records are faulty. We do not think that your suggestion to send Piobán McPludaire to the Escorial would serve any useful purpose during these troubled times.

Your barrel of poteen delighted Our court dwarf and he induced Us to take a sip. We must say regretfully that it did not agree with Us and We suffered a Royal Indisposition. This caused Us to be ill over the corridors of the Escorial. Help at present is impossible. We do not think that Our army would survive the rigours of your climate. However, We have sent you four hundred barrels of good Spanish wine and ordered them to be left for you on Aisling pier at Inis Orga, from where Our sailors have been instructed to carry home the famous Inis Orga lobster and oysters. When you tap the barrels and drink the wine, think kindly of the Troubled Monarch of Spain. We trust that this letter will render unnecessary any further correspondence. We hope that Our reluctance to send troops in no way hampers your preparations for war,
Sincerely yours,
The King of Spain.

——The bloody traitor. Nothing but words, a voice commented.
——Ireland has no friends in her hour of need, another moaned.
——It's not what the hoor said but what he didn't say, a third voice added.
——It's put an end to our dreams of establishing a Celtic Ireland. Baile will now never be taken, someone else told

them.

—We would need an army inside Baile to take it, an adviser said. And we have no friends in Baile.

—Then we'll have to wait and fight another day, Murtagh told them readily.

With these final words, he terminated the feast which was held at the Castle of Skattery, in the Barony of Skattery which had uncertain boundaries.

Murtagh McMurtagh lay in conjunction with his neighbour's wife during October. This was his divine right as Prince of Skattery. It was a right more honoured in the observance than in the breach. So men were careful with their wives. On fair days in the small town the women folk were hidden from his gaze for he had a wandering eye, a quick lust. He had never married and there was no legitimate heir.

—If he put half the effort into fighting as he does to dropping bastards, then England would be ruled from Ireland and the House of Commons would be the Castle of Skattery, the chieftains commented. But if he died in the morning nine hundred could claim his crown, they added.

—I'll get married when the time comes, boys. Don't hurry me for I'm still a young man. One must be cautious in these matters and choose well.

—But you have been cautious. 'Tis not that you haven't had the opportunity to know married and unmarried women. We must avoid scandal.

—Am I not protected by the divine right of kings? Not even the Pope can change that.

—And what if the power leaves you suddenly?

—Whatever power leaves me, boys, it's one power that won't.

The power had not left him when he lay in conjunction with Nell Hogan in October. They lay under a thatch of badly-cured sheep skins, tributes from the sub-tribes of his kingdom. Each sheep skin carried the character of a particular tribe. By his bed stood a sword, shield, and helmet, in the event of his being called to war.

—Will there be war, Murtagh? she asked him.

—What do you mean?

—The whole kingdom is buzzing, like a hive of bees ready to swarm, with rumours.

—There will be no war. This is not the time of year. If an army were to march in or out of the barony at this moment it would lodge itself in a bog.

—What do I mean to you, Murtagh?

—You mean more to me, Nell, than ten of the finest milking cows in Munster, and they give great milk.

—An', Murtagh, there has been no bull to compare with you since Maeve sent the men in search of the great Bull of Cooley. You even smell like a bull.

He had a matted chest of hair, thick as goat hide, and the sweat under his oxters had been fermenting for six months. He proved that the mythical and agricultural allusions were true. The castle shook from each ceiling to each floor as he exercised the divine right of kings.

Scribo Lynch the Scribe rushed up the winding stairs to the penthouse and knocked upon the door.

—Who's there? Murtagh asked.

—Scribo.

—Did I call you?

—I heard you yell.

—Quick, get down between my feet and nobody will know that you are there at all, he told Nell.

Resting her head between his stiff and sweat-caked stockings she listened.

—Enter, Murtagh ordered.

He entered with pen and parchment. Amanuensis to Murtagh McMurtagh, who was illiterate, Scribo told him that they had firm information that his brother, Cormac MacMurtagh, in Baile asylum, was planning a rebellion. He intended to overpower the town and establish a French republic there.

—Take a letter, Murtagh ordered, sitting up in the bed and placing his hands upon his chest and interlocking his fingers.

> Dear Cormac of the Bright Mind.
>
> Greetings. I hope you have received the bag of potatoes, the flour, the box of snuff and the tobacco which I sent to you at the asylum. I hope also that you are in good health and that the great pain at the back of your skull is not causing any trouble.
>
> The weather in the barony is very bad and it put the crops back by five weeks. The turf and the potatoes are wet, we can look forward to a dismal winter.
>
> But it is now time to talk of rebellion. It has come to our ears that you contemplate war

and that active preparations are in progress. Like you, we intend to take the town of Baile and we would like to join in an alliance with you. As you know, blood is thicker than water and the McMurtagh blood is very thick. It is time now to bury our difference.

During the last months I've been training troops. Each morning at seven o'clock the tribes assemble in the courtyard and carry out the various drills. I have ordered a replica of Baile to be built from turf in the bog; the sod town is directly under the castle. We scale the walls, set the public buildings on fire, hang all traitors and drive the whores of Berwick Square into the convent . . .

—-But we don't, Scribo said.

—-I know. The idea has just come to me and it is a bright idea. When the letter has been dispatched get every able-bodied man to build a replica of Baile in front of the castle so that I can direct the war from the bed.

—-As you command.

—-Now let's continue.

Perhaps we differ in small political ways. It is time to settle these differences. There will be plenty of land to go around when the time comes to divide it and you can set up your French republic wherever you wish. I have a great regard for the French way of life. For too long Ireland has been cut off from the continent of Europe. Our immediate object, however, should be to rid the country of foreign usurpers. I hope that you find my plans agreeable. Write when you can.

Sincerely yours,
Murtagh McMurtagh, Prince of the Barony
of Skattery.

Scribo finished writing with a professional whirl of his pen, then held it above the parchment and plunged it down to inflict a final dot.

—-Well, what do you think of that for a letter? There's talk for you, Murtagh boasted.

—-It's good. But I thought you said that we would give our blood only for Ireland, now we will be spilling it for Ireland and France.

——It's military strategy. Sure, when we have taken the town we'll drive all Cormac's army back to the asylum where they belong, or maybe float them out to sea in that ark that Noah McNulty is building to take him to Byzantium.

——I see. And with that he left.

——So you are going to war, Nell said, coming up from her unhappy position between his feet.

——Come spring, Nell. Nobody ever went to war in winter. Imagine how cold it would be lying on a field of trampled snow, your blood hard frozen. A man might not get a chance to spill his blood for Ireland if it were frozen into him.

——I remember when I was a comely maiden waiting for you all to march down the road to Baile.

——And we did in the years '67 and '68.

——But when you got down to the crossroads you turned back.

——It was the weather, Nell. The weather came against us.

They built the town to his specifications in front of the castle. They erected walls of turf, a cathedral of turf, an asylum of turf, a pier leading to a bog hole. From his position on the battlements Murtagh could direct military activity.

At the beginning of each week the town was taken and raised to the ground; traitors were hanged and Anna Morphy and her whores were driven into the convent. By Sunday the town was built again. But the McMurtaghs knew in their narrow hearts that the conquest would be no easy matter. Imagine as they would, and their imaginations were of the highest Celtic quality, turf was turf and no flight of fancy could turn it into stone. The stuffed bags hanging from the gibbets had neither tongue, nor heart, nor cause. And the old women who played the parts of the fancy-women of Baile did not compare with the inhabitants of Berwick Square. It would be an easy thing to send Skattery women to a nunnery, and to keep them there. But the descriptions of Anna Morphy which had trickled into the barony were such that the men would rather keep her out of a nunnery than imprison her there.

The mock military activity did have some advantages. It sharpened the rusty war cries of the McMurtaghs. It beat sub-tribes into regiments. It exercised the spavined horses and created a certain interest in things during the months of January and February. The tribes learned about military positions, the call to arms, the orders to advance and retreat, regroup, readvance and reretreat. By February they had a thirst for battle, something which Murtagh had not foreseen.

—I'll be forced into war, he told his neighbour's wife, when spring was coming and grass starting to grow in the battlement gutters.

—There will be no turning back this time, Nell replied.

—It seems so. I should never have built a turf town. I thought I was satisfying one desire and instead I kindled another. I thought that when they took Baile, vicariously, they would forget that a real stone town existed. Now they want to march out of the barony against the congregated might of England. And worse still, they have got a taste for loose women.

He paced up and down the floor, looking out the small window east and looking out the small window west. He might die on the field of battle and no Murtagh McMurtagh to ascend the throne.

—Things are looking bad, Nell. They never looked worse. I'll be forced to marry.

—It is an easy step. You can be the father of as many inside marriage as you are outside.

—I know, Nell, but I have to meet the right woman.

—And what about myself? Wouldn't I suit you inch for inch and yard for yard, and am I not equal to your grass?

—I'll think about it, Nell. I'll think about it. I can only marry you if your husband dies in battle. I'll have to put him in the front line.

There was a loud roar far beneath them as the McMurtaghs took Baile.

—I'm tired of taking clamps of turf, Nestor McMurtagh said, while the great chief is up there in the top of the castle, his backside warm, his belly full, his anguish satisfied, and the rest of us frostbitten and rheumy.

—He should be hung by the nails of his toes, Bluster McMurtagh said. He's no good to either man or beast.

—You men could be hung for treason, an old one told them. Murtagh up there is a fierce man in battle.

—He was never in a battle.

—But you heard him talk about what he would do on the glorious day. Another thing, he's the only man who has an overall view of the fight and he can give the orders correctly.

Dissatisfaction was growing among the young bloods and blades. Already Traitor McMurtagh had smuggled information out of the barony which was now in the War Office. In London they thought that the situation was potentially dangerous. It was the first time that Murtagh McMurtagh had assembled a proper army.

They looked at the large map of their troubled Empire. Troops had been deployed on all its eastern borders. It would be impossible to rush crack troops to Baile in the event of an uprising in Skattery.

Cormac McMurtagh read his brother's letter in his private room at the asylum of Baile. Herod-minded, his brother could destroy him. But he had plans. He would have Murtagh and the other McMurtagh leaders immured in the asylum. He would destroy the old traditions and bring Continental ideas into the barony. Hackett the Harper and Piobán McPludaire must die.

——The old poets must die, he often said to himself when he was taking his own counsel. And new poets must be born. They can be the greatest friends or the greatest enemies to any revolution.

He sat before the fire, an ornamental sword between his legs, and gave these ideas much thought. He sipped the Spanish wine which had been brought from Inis Orga and there discovered the contours and the colours of France upon his tongue. He wondered if the vine would strike roots in Irish soil.

He considered Inis Orga. He had not decided what he would do with the island when the revolution was successful. Should he send a punitive expedition there? Should he sign a treaty with Tostach Joyce, the chief poet of the island? Should he turn it into a penal colony?

There was a knock upon the door.

——Who goes there? he asked.

——Citizen Murphy, the voice replied.

——Entrez.

——Bonsoir, Murphy said on entering.

——Bonsoir to you, citizen. Take a seat.

Citizen Murphy sat down. He looked into the fire. There was the deep trace of anguish on his face.

——Are you suffering from Continental anguish or just local anguish, Citizen Murphy?

——Local anguish. I'm having doubts about the revolution.

——Are preparations not running smoothly?

——Very smoothly. Mucus Daly and Koola Akibu continue

to dig up uniforms. Sadie Vaughan has the women in good order. I worry though what we will do with the bishops of Ireland.

—I'll lock the whole lot of them up, along with whatever cardinals I come across.

—Surely you won't lock up the Wandering Friar?

—I'll make him an ambassador.

—He deserves such an honour. And Noah McNulty?

—I will make him Patriarch of Baile.

—My mind is at rest. I feared the bishops.

—I have let nothing to chance. Now that you see everything as it shall be, I'll invite you to sip a glass of French wine.

—It doesn't agree with my stomach.

—Well, you'll have to drink it when the revolution comes.

—If that is so, I might as well start now.

Cormac McMurtagh poured the Spanish wine. Citizen Murphy lodged it in his stomach.

—It's a good French wine, citizen. When you get to know your wines you will discover that each one has a special bouquet and by taste alone you can tell the exact place in France from whence it came. It is our great link with the Republic.

—The geography in wine is remarkable. Citizen Murphy gulped another mouthful of wine and inwardly cursed the French soil from which it had sprung.

—Sip it, citizen.

—To tell the truth, Cormac, it's rat poison.

—It is an acquired taste. I got it through reading revolutionary literature.

Their minds turned from wine to the war.

—The coming revolution has put great spirit into us all, Cormac. It has given life and aim. Fellows that were sitting around wearing the arse off their trousers, waiting for death, have got new heart and most of them can now count to ten in French.

—I know what I am doing, Citizen Murphy.

—It was surely a great idea, dividing everything into tenths.

—It's logical, citizen. We have ten fingers and ten toes.

—But giving every tenth a colour was the best idea of all.

—My idea, he lied.

It was late now. The warders, having finished playing poker in the front office, made a final check on the corridors and dormitories. The building was as quiet as a convent.

——This must be the best run asylum in Ireland, Warder Garvey said to a companion. It's strange that from ten on-wards there is not the suggestion of a sound and it has been like that since Cormac McMurtagh decided to put on a musical.

Not knowing that the year of the revolution was at hand they went to bed.

Mucus Daly and Koola Akibu left their beds at the twelfth stroke of the Protestant clock. They took shovels from under their mattresses of rush, whispered *Vive La Republique* to each other and moved in the direction of the women's quarters. Sadie Vaughan opened the door for the two men and allowed them into the forbidden corridors.

——I can smell the flesh of women everywhere, Koola Akibu said.

——Caution your desires, warned Mucus.

——I can smell the flesh of women everywhere, he said again, taking a deep breath.

——He's a pagan, Sadie. He'll have to be haltered, or maybe worse.

——Think of the revolution, she told them.

——Any word of corpses? Mucus asked.

——There have been two funerals today. One at the Pro-testant cemetery and one at the Catholic one.

——That means two more uniforms. Who were they? Mucus asked.

——One was a widow, five times married. Five wedding rings were buried with her.

——A good night's takings there.

——Work quickly and get back here without notice.

——Koola Akibu, being black, is part of the night and gives no reflection, said Mucus.

——I smell the flesh and the sweat of women.

Sadie Vaughan would be in charge of the women's brigade when the fighting began. She had worked with Florence Nightingale at Balaclava. She had been witness to the winter snows on the Russian hills and the charge of the Light Brigade. On her return to Baile she had been honoured by the town councillors. Then they forgot about her until she started walking the streets, lamp in hand, looking for the military dead. They placed her in the asylum where she often walked the corridors looking for the bodies of the military dead.

From the outset she had agreed with the thoughts of Cormac McMurtagh which had been circulated through the asylum in the Small Yellow Manuscript. His ideas were cold, ordered, mathematical, like the moves in a chess game. Once she had Cormac accept the basic tenet that all men and women are equal she accepted all the actions which followed. She had drawn the attention of Cormac to the existence of women in the asylum. She had prompted him to change the basic tenet in his little Yellow Manuscript to include women. The manuscripts were recalled and the first statement was altered from 'all men are equal' to the more inclusive one, 'all men and women are equal differently'.

To her was given the task of clothing the revolutionaries. Her plan was simple.

—If everything is to be divided in tenths, as you suggest in your Small Yellow Manuscript, then every regiment should have its own colour. In this way the men will know where they belong. They may not understand commands but they understand colours. And every man will have a ribbon tied around his toe, coloured with the dye of his regiment. It will be the first thing he sees getting up in the morning and the last thing he sees going to bed at night. And every colour should have a function.

—That's a great idea, but now we have to get uniforms.

—Dig them up, Cormac, dig them up. We'll dig up every corpse the night of the day it is buried, take the shroud and dye it to whatever colour you wish.

Now she had sufficient shrouds to clothe eight of the ten regiments. They hung in the vaults in rows of grass-green, soup-grey, tea-brown, whin-yellow, sloe-purple, leper-white, funeral-black, and blood-red. It remained only to dig up two more regiments of shrouds and dye them ashpit-ochre and peeler-blue.

—We must have five hundred uniforms? Mucus Daly asked her.

—That's a military secret. Think only of the Republic. All men and women will be free, the heads of large and small tyrants will be severed by Pat Gilfoyle's guillotine and fall into the large sally baskets we are making.

—Night and day we're dreaming of it, Sadie.

—Follow me.

Her lamp showed the two travelling shadows to the small gate through which they would all eventually escape, surround the asylum and call on it to surrender.

With their shovels upon their backs, they stepped through the gate and out into the unreliable world of sanity. It was a sharp night. The stars were in place, well polished and in good order. A clear-eyed moon minimally lit up the world.

—A good night for digging corpses, Mucus remarked. There is clear vision and no rain. I hate nights when the ground is mucky and we have to dirty the dead.

—It's good to get them on the night of the day they die. I'll never forget the night we dug up the six-week-old grave. I almost vomited, Koola said.

—Yes. Flesh melting from bones is a terribly distressing sight.

They headed by the back roads of the town to the Protestant cemetery with its ordered dead, comfortable inscriptions and well-kept paths.

—And remember, Mucus Daly said to Koola, if we are in an exposed place and the moonlight is strong, I'll stand behind a yew tree and light my pipe while you do the digging.

They climbed over the stile. A solid, square chapel squatted under the trees like a guard dog. The moon looked out from each window as they went by. They walked behind the church and saw no moons at all.

—It proves that the moon has a black backside like myself.

They walked between the ordered slabs, tables of stone, pillered urns. They could read the tombstone incriptions by the slanted light.

—'Here lieth the body of Tobias Smith, resting after the battles of life', Koola chanted solemnly.

—Grand. Lieth is a comfortable word, Tobias a Biblical one.

—Here's one that resteth, Koola pointed at another slab. What a place to rest.

They went in search of the Protestant widow's grave. They found earth turned in a quiet corner.

—She was five times married, Mucus told Koola. She must have the stamina of a jennit.

They took off their coats, opened their waistcoats, lubricated their hands with sputum, and began. Working together for two years, they had developed a rhythmic pattern. They hummed republican tunes while they threw up the earth in easy spadefuls. The night was a rectangle of stars above them.

—Easy. Easy now, Mucus directed when they reached the final inch of earth. Finger back the clay. I wouldn't like to dinge the brass plate.

They eased back the clay from the coffin plate and from the screws.

——Get the screwdriver and remove the screws, Mucus told Koola.

He screwed them off and handed them to Mucus.

——More screws for the ark. If the revolution fails and the deluge comes, Noah McNulty has promised us a place in the boat, Mucus said.

They opened the door of death and there she lay, five rings on her married fingers.

——She's well turned out and there is still a rich smell from her flesh, Mucus remarked. Get her up into a standing position and I'll hitch the shroud over her head.

Koola held the dead woman in a lover's embrace and Mucus hitched up the shroud.

It must have been the sting of the cold on her backside which woke her from the coma. She opened her eyes and looked at Mucus Daly.

——Rape! she cried.

——The saints of Ireland preserve us, Mucus called and jumped on to the lip of the grave. Koola scampered up after him. They grabbed their spades and rushed from the foreign plot.

——It's right what they say on the tombstones. Some Protestants are not dead at all but only lieth, panted Koola.

The Protestant widow straightened her hair, brushed the creases out of her shroud, climbed out of her grave and walked home.

Mucus Daly and Koola Akibu took refuge in the Catholic cemetery. Their sinews were soft, their faces grey.

——I'll never be the same again, Mucus gasped.

——And I've turned white.

——It's a bad business we're in, Mucus said when his sinews had hardened. I don't feel like turning another spadeful tonight.

——We must.

The moon was quiet. It lit the tangled paths of the grave-yard. They discovered fresh earth. They had less respect for the Catholic dead than the Protestant dead, perhaps because they brought their poverty with them and had cheap shrouds. They quickly dug the grave, recovered some screws for the ark and knocked the coffin lid to splinters.

——Be cripes! said Mucus Daly. But if it isn't the corpse of

Christy Gavin.

—Did you know him?

—Know him! I knew him well, Koola. He was the wittiest man in town. He had a thousand jokes. I don't know how many times he carried me around the kitchen on his back. Ah, but he was the boy that could set the pub roaring. And look at him now. Not a word to say, not a single word.

—I suppose Napoleon looked like this in his grave.

—Ah, and Henry the Eighth and Alexander.

They robbed Christy of his shroud. They piled the earth back carelessly. Then they made their way out of the grave-yard.

They returned to the asylum. By now Cormac McMurtagh was deep in wine-sleep and Citizen Murphy vomiting vinegar.

There was only one buckle in the soundness of Cormac McMurtagh's mind. He confused the municipal town of Baile with the city of Paris on the eve of the French Revolution and he thought that he was Citizen Robespierre. When he looked down upon the rooftops from his angular garret he heard only the confusion of streets, the cries of merchants and aristocrats as they were drawn in horse carts towards the guillotine.

—There must be disorder before we have order and blood must be spilt so that blood will not be spilt again, he often told his lieutenants when they stood about his deal table and listened to the plans for his revolution.

—Each man has a function to fulfil. He was created to serve the State in some way or other. When he does this the State is healthy and he is happy. Positions in a State are not inherited. They are earned.

He told his lieutenants many other things as they stood about him during the winter months and planned the con-quest of Baile. When the revolution was successful words spoken in the angular garret would be inscribed on ten slabs of granite and placed in the square of Baile where all could read them in French. They were to be called The Ten Slabs of Wisdom.

The lunatic asylum was a well-proportioned building. The length was balanced by the height, windows by doors and garrets subservient to the general proportion.

Cormac could never be certain when he discovered that only a revolution based on tenths could be a successful one.

—We have ten fingers and ten toes, he argued. And this

alone is significant proof that the harmony of the world is
based on tens and tenths. There must be ten seconds in a
minute, minutes in an hour, hours in a day, days in a week,
weeks in a month and months in a year. The pendulums of all
clocks will be slowed down to get the correct second length
and upon this time measure the whole system will be based.
Instead of going tick-tock the clocks will have to go tuck-
tack. Once we have the clocks tucking correctly then the
whole harmony of work and play will be built around it.

The lieutenants had to agree that this was a great and new
idea. From his principle of tenths he worked out his divisions
of all conquered towns. They would be divided into tenths
and these tenths would be divided into tenths and these in
their turn also into tenths.

The garret was the womb of the revolution. Here stood his
chair, his sword, his cockade, the autobiography of Rousseau
and republican literature. He had a turf fire, a good supply of
wine and a large French dictionary. His brother, Murtagh,
subsidised this extravagance and thus maintained his throne
in peace.

At the sound of the night bell he donned his cockade, put
on his military uniform, buckled on his sword belt and
opened a bottle of wine. At this hour he took his pen in hand
and continued writing his memoirs. At eleven he rang a small
desk bell and waited for his lieutenant, Citizen Casey, to
report on the events of the day.

There were ten lieutenants, the Chosen Ten, each with a
colour and responsibilities: Murphy, grass-green, in charge
of agriculture; Walsh, soup-grey, in charge of soup kitchens;
Wallace, blood-red, military courts, ammunition, prisons and
the guillotine; Durcan, whin-yellow, education, propaganda,
the printing press, French and morals; Bellow, tea-brown,
road works and public servants; Kilcoyne, sloe-purple, in
charge of sanity and shipping; Hamrock, leper-white, military hospitals; Deegan, funeral-black, responsible for burying
the dead; Higgins, ashpit-ochre, in charge of art, monuments,
the striking of medals and military music; Casey, peeler-blue,
law enforcement.

Citizen Casey entered, dressed in a peeler's uniform taken
from a grave. He bowed from the waist, shouted *Vive La
Republique*! and began his recitation.

——Foley of Belahy has died; a carpenter is lost to the
revolution. The troops complain that the porridge is rotten,
the soup sour; this might generate a rebellion and not a

revolution. The fighting men in Citizen Murphy's unit now stand at ninety-two; they are totally armed with stolen brush handles and live in the expectation of pike-heads. Iron plough shares have been smuggled in from Baile and are presently being beaten into swords. Lead has been safely stolen from the Protestant Church and hardened into oval blunderbuss bullets; the art of casting circular blunderbuss bullets has not yet been successful. There are unsubstantiated rumours that many of the inmates have funded Noah McNulty's ark, in the hope of securing safe passage in the event of a deluge. There is a more substantial rumour that help is on its way from Spain to Murtagh McMurtagh. A black man of huge proportions called Pádraigh Gorm na Mara now lives with Tostach Joyce on Inis Orga and speaks real Irish. The inmates wonder if a day and date has been set for the revolution. The troops complain that the porridge is rotten and the milk sour; this might generate a rebellion and not a revolution.

——Why did you repeat the second point twice?

——I had only nine points and I wished to bring the number up to ten.

——Smart thinking, Citizen Casey. You may be President of the Republic some day.

All the lieutenants were later drawn together about a map.

——The revolution is almost at hand, Cormac McMurtagh began. Here is a new map of Baile. It is divided up into ten coloured segments and each of these in turn is subdivided into ten. When the revolution comes, as come it will, set up a commune in your tenth, and fly your coloured flag from the tallest chimney. Each commune must have a jail. Comandeer a public-house, paint out the owner's name, as everything will belong to everybody, and put the word jail in its place. That is the way a public-house is changed into a jail. A courier must be dispatched from each commune, on an ass, to headquarters with the accounts of various battles so that I can follow the progress. A file must be kept on all actions so that we will have original sources for our historians who will sit and write the story.

——There are certain buildings in the town marked for closure. The Convent of the Large Sisters of Saint Vitas will be turned into a school for retraining the women of Baile. Here they will learn carding, knitting, weaving, flag and cockade making. The Order of the Large Sisters of Saint Vitas will be disbanded. The sisters will be given the opportunity of staying on in Baile if they take the oath of allegiance and wear secular dress. The Little Black Brothers will be rounded up and put in a barge which will be scuttled in the bay. Their monastery will be converted into a wine depot, where the wines of republican France will be stored.

—Madame Anna Morphy will be the new Goddess of Reason. She will be installed in the council chambers, in semi-transparencies, and will strike classical poses. She will also read our Declaration of Independence in French.

—And the other Berwick Square whores?

—They will serve under the soldiers.

There was communal approval in this matter.

—The official language of the revolution will be French.

—Who will teach us French?

—The Goddess of Reason herself, he replied.

—It's a very hard tongue to manage, Citizen Durcan said.

—Haven't you already picked up the most difficult words in Vive la République, bonsoir, fraternité, égalité et liberté?

—We have.

—Well, keep roaring them as you move from place to place, so everybody will think we are acquainted with the language.

—A terrible beauty will certainly be born.

—The new catechism of the Republic will be the Little Yellow Book which contains my thoughts.

· —Without such thoughts, Cormac, things would fall apart, the centre would not hold.

—My thoughts on property are well known. Eventually all houses will be pulled down and the model houses built in Baile. Each one will have two storeys, a slated roof, six windows and two doors. All furniture, delph and beds will be standard. In the kitchen of every model house will hang my portrait, close to a clock which will go tuck-tack. This means that everybody will be at home anywhere at every moment. That is all, citizens.

—I forgot to mention that we discovered two brass cannons today, Citizen Wallace said. While the men were digging the latrines. But we have no cannonballs, sir.

—Haven't we turnips! Coat the turnips with lead and what have you got?

—Cannonballs a size bigger than turnips.

—Any more problems?

—The guillotine. The coffin maker has already made a preliminary model. He has decapitated ten hens but he doubts if he can build one big enough or sharp enough to cut off heads. He thinks that he will have to give two runs to each head.

——Have a larger guillotine built immediately for testing. You cannot have a revolution without a guillotine. Revolutionary tribunal, dismissed!

——Vive la République! Bonsoir, liberté, égalité, fraternité, liberté, bonsoir, fraternité! The Chosen Ten said and departed.

——Fine men, fine men, Citizen McMurtagh said. Men that the sane world cannot well do without!

He sipped his French wine, broke some rough cheese and masticated it, standing before the garret window which looked down upon Baile. He practised his address to the liberated.

——To conquer we have need to dare, and dare again. Baile will be free. What care I for reputation. What care I, if I am called a blood drinker. There is nothing immutable save reason, save the sovereignty of the people. Live free, or die.

Below him the town was torched, the cobbles blooded. He was carted through the street in Humper Donaghue's barrow. Before him stood the guillotine. The revolution was eating its young and its middle-aged. Anna Morphy was knitting socks before the large sally basket. His head was on the block. There were ten familiar heads in the basket. He blinded his eyes to the vision.

Somewhere in the distance Noah McNulty was hammering.

CHAPTER FOUR

By spring the rumour had travelled down all the roads of the world. It took sail and passed beneath the Capes. It split, duplicated and grew.

By February the price of Inis Orga lobsters and oysters had surpassed the expectation of the poets. Arab pirates had anchored in Barra Bay, enduring the cold of winter, the curved gales and the steep seas. Pádraigh Gorm na Mara, for sizeable creels of gold, piloted ships to oyster beds and lobster haunts. For thirty sovereigns he sold bottles of poteen.

By March the poets had forty creels of gold, some sorted in barrels, some in the settle and some in the potato pits.

—People will believe anything, Tostach Joyce told them.

They had no clear notion in their minds what to do with all the gold which Pádraigh brought into the kitchen.

—Put it in the stack of turf, they said. —The stack of turf is already filled. —Put it in the potato pit. —That's filled. —Try the bog hole. —That's filled. —Plug the stone walls. —I will, but they will be quickly filled. —Well, plug them anyway and maybe tomorrow we'll find somewhere else to put it.

They brought their minds back to the serious business of poetry. No sooner had they begun to think of verse than their minds were on the heaps of gold which lay in potato pits, bog holes, the outhouse and in stone walls.

—It's a pity to let it go to waste, Celibate said. It will rot on us.

—Gold is useless unless you use it. We might as well have a cart of stones outside the door, Gub Keogh told them.

—It's a bothersome thing, Duck Flaherty said.

—We are not used to it, like titled people or landed

75

gentry. That's our trouble, Tostach Joyce remarked. I suggest that we leave this forsaken island, which is nothing more than a rock covered with a wet straw. We'll go off to Dublin where the weather is warm, the streets metalled and carriages are drawn by white horses. There we can have anything we ever wanted. What is poetry, but the refuge of the poor and the oppressed.

——Maybe we could go to London and live close to the Queen, among the nobility, Duck Flaherty said.

——Or go to Italy and see the Pope, Celibate Corcoran suggested.

——No, I think we should retire to the rooms of Madame Anna Morphy, Amorous said. There, all desires are satisfied.

——I'm all for investing some of it in rare wines, The Yellow Gunner informed them.

——Put it into a castle, Stone Ryan suggested. We could have our ease there, a suitable housing for the great bed, and servants to attend us.

——No, land is the place to put money, Stitcher Sweeney told them. Land lasts almost forever.

——Stop! roared Tostach Joyce. You are destroying yourselves. They would not understand your Irish in Dublin and you would look awkward on the high streets with your island walk. And the Queen has no desire to see you. In Rome you would have to speak Italian and do so as the Romans, and the Pope has more to do with his time than entertain island poets. In Madame Anna Morphy's you would pick up gunnery. Invest in French wines and you will kill yourselves before the year is out. If you leave the island you will be out of the sound of the sea . . .

The Yellow Gunner interjected, ——I hate all the caution. I want what's coming to me. I'll write no more poetry.

——And what about that great poem of yours?

——I've written it. It's at the back of my head and it's the greatest poem ever written in Inis Orga since time began.

——Recite it, they challenged.

——I won't. And I might never recite it. But I know I did what I was born to do, and all I wish to do now is to drink.

There was long oblong silence, three yards by five.

——He's a disgrace, they all said.

——Here we are, with more money than the King of Sheba and it's of no use to us. We got it too fast. If it had come in small sums, like in the letters from America, we could have bought an ass, or a cow, or a second boat. It's a bad thing when it comes in creels, Mackerel Malone told them.

——We could give it to a parish priest or maybe to the Bishop, Celibate Corcoran suggested.

——No, I won't give money to the Church. We might corrupt the clergy and none of us want to have that on our consciences, replied Pat the Pagan.

——It's a bad thing to corrupt the clergy, they all agreed.

——Let us remain silent and think about it, Tostach Joyce directed.

——And while you are, I'll recite my poem, in case I might die and carry it with me to the grave, The Gunner said.

——Go ahead, they told him, breaking the silence.

He drank from his mug of wine and harrowed phlegm from his throat.

Before he had finished the poem the poets of Inis Orga knew that The Yellow Gunner had achieved what they all wished to achieve, immortality. They nodded their approval and that was the greatest honour they could confer upon him.

——Leave me alone now. I'm thirsty and I want a drink.

He turned from them, gulped a large mouthful of wine, gathered himself together and fell asleep.

After much thought, and much later, the poets decided what they would do with the gold: they would build a new, spacious cottage in the likeness of a Greek temple and in it they would place the Great French Whore's bed; they would send money to their poor relations in America; they would sustain hungry poets and writers in distant countries; they would import marble from Italy for Stone Ryan; they would build a stone forum where every man could have his say; they would purchase Inis Orga from the Queen and declare it a republic; they would endow lectureships, devoted to the poets of Inis Orga, at Cambridge, Oxford and Dublin University; the rest of the money they would bury in the bog and set Irish wolfhounds to guard it.

——That's the best use money can be put to, Tostach Joyce told them, and they put their spit of approval on it.

Noah McNulty by sea-lantern light began to plank the deck of the ark. With the deck laid the boat in its general features would be complete. At its centre, like an island and stilted, stood the cabin, where he often slept. On his arrival at that golden city he intended to linger only a short time. Then, following the custom he had read of in Syrian hagiography, he would seek complete seclusion on top of some ancient pillar. He was familiar with the life of Saint Daniel of Samosata, who had spent forty-two years on a pillar, and would simulate him.

He looked into the depths of the ark, half-discovered by the lantern light. The moon was mirrored on the pool of water there, along with half the stars in the Plough. It was a tiresome occupation, bailing out the boat. However, the half-continuous rain tested the caulking of the boat. Up to a certain level it was water-tight from the inside.

What should he take from Baile as a testament to a submerged town, he asked in the sober part of his mind which dealt with reality. Many objects had been canvassed but none were durable and inclusive. Finally he settled upon the Crusader's headstone, chiselled during the Black Death. It showed the lord and his lady, desiccated flesh upon bone, his skull with crusader's helmet, her skull with nunnish wimple. This he would carry to Byzantium, a fair city to the east and not shown upon the pilgrim maps.

However, he was short of money. He had had recourse to base means of procuring it, he thought as he screwed a plank into place. He had raised the Spanish Friar to the See of Nubia, anointing him with the oil which, it was claimed, had flowed down the beard of Moses' brother, Aaron. Unfortunately, it was only the oil which had flowed down the beard of Solomon and the See of Nubia had been promised to another.

He could finish his wide deck if he had gold but there was no longer gold in abundance, not even from the municipal councillors; he had sold all the Sees he would govern from his stylite when he reached the fabled land somewhere in the east, bordering on an inland sea untroubled by tides.

To his certain knowledge, and sometimes he could be certain of knowledge, there was only one source of gold and that was to the west, on the misty island of Inis Orga. Already foreign traders had left their gold with the poets. He knew something of the poets and he decided upon a plan.

So, one night he took a small boat, hoisted the sail and set out for the island.

The poets, unaware of his approach, lay in the wide bed. Pádraigh Gorm na Mara brought them potatoes from the pit and fish from the porter-dark sea. The milk, thin, was laced with poteen to give it body.

During these months Stone Ryan often left the bed, took his Grecian mallet and Grecian chisel, and chipped at the marble statue. He worked evenly and the woman was drawn slowly from the primal stone. She was the vision that poets saw in dream woods.

—Venus, speak to us, the poets often said.

—She will send all the men of Gawna to hell, Celibate Corcoran told them.

—They are already on the way there, Duck Flaherty answered.

—It will help them on.

—They deserve such help!

—She is like the Greek maidens I met in Arcadia, Amorous Aynsworth said. A sweet memory of days of dalliance in Arcadia.

—Before or after the Greek thief stole your trousers?

—Fortunately, afterwards.

—I'm moving to the far end of the bed, Celibate Corcoran told them. He emerged from the large quilt and walked across the bed to the other end, out of vision of Venus.

As the statue continued to grow, so did their wonder and admiration. There were many critical remarks generated by her advent from stone. The expression on the face was noted; words were put into the statue's mouth. The fingers were counted and measured and found accurate. They admired the sensitivity with which the hands were aligned in the interests of modesty. Her age was a matter of opinion. Her attitude was compared and contrasted with the woman in oak at the end of the bed.

—She's a bad yoke, that one at the end of the bed, Mackerel Malone said, looking at her above the row of caps. And carved with evil intent. Stone Ryan's statue could stand in any city square.

—Ireland is not ready for such statues, they had to admit.

—He would be better engaged carving statues of Saint Patrick or Saint Joseph, Celibate Corcoran declared. It would engage the good opinion of the bishops and parish priests.

—I did a statue of Saint Patrick once and I was plagued by a parish priest, Stone Ryan replied. He wasn't satisfied by the beard or by the mitre and he wanted a serpent on the crozier. So finally we argued upon the matter and I knocked the head off the statue and left that part of Ireland, putting the mason's curse upon it.

——And what was the curse?

——May a writer called James Joyce be born here and write a book called *Ulysses*!

——Stop the rameis, The Yellow Gunner said. What do you know? You never travelled. Were any of you ever in Africa?

——No.

——I was, and I was in the islands of the south, and I think that we were all born naked and were intended to stay naked, but we got used to clothes.

——I would agree with that, Amorous Aynsworth said.

——That's enough, the others told them. You have gone too far. Arguments can be carried too far.

——I thought this was a democracy? The Yellow Gunner asked.

——And so it is.

——That means I am free to speak?

——You are free to speak as long as you don't go too far, and you have gone too far.

——I have not.

——You have, and also you are unclear of mind.

——Stone Ryan would be far better engaged in making a statue of me, with a yellow bittern at my feet.

——Only saints and beautiful women are fit subjects for the carver's hand, they told him.

——Whose voice do you quote?

——The voice of tradition.

——I'm tired of tradition. If he made a true statue of me and placed the bittern at my feet, and the two of us at a crossroads, then those who looked upon it might be stirred to a little sympathy for wayward men and ugly birds, instead of chasing us from pub doors and taking our good name from pulpits.

As the sailboat carrying Noah McNulty approached the island, Stone Ryan lay down his Greek mallet and Greek chisel and declared the statue finished. Venus was finally released from stone. She stood, finished, in the half-light of the fire and the quarter-light of the day. She was the first Venus ever born upon Inis Orga.

——Open the door and light the candles, Tostach Joyce directed. We have only seen the statue in half-light. Maybe it's flawed in some way.

They left the bed and each took a candle and stood before the statue. Then they moved about it, blowing puffs of smoke from pouted lips.

From the south, the north, the east and the west, it was perfect. It was the most glorious thing their eyes had ever lit upon, other than the sight of the setting sun, or the moon with a sharp frost edge, or the precision of the stars

—Some have it in their feet for dancing, but, Stone Ryan, you have it in your hands for carving, they told him.

—No matter what Celibate Corcoran says, Pagan Pat declared, this woman has no scratch upon her. She's not brazen like the one at the foot of the bed.

—I don't know, I don't know. You have me moidered with all this thought. I have my doubts. This is a damp and cold climate. He should have left a skirt on her.

They mused upon the wondrous statue for two hours and then they returned to the bed, where they were served mugs of tea.

Having moored his boat, Noah McNulty made his way along the sheep paths to the cottage set in the palm of two hungry hills. He knocked on the door.

—See if it's an Arabian with gold, Tostach Joyce told Pádraigh Gorm na Mara.

He opened the door and looked at the ascetical face of Noah McNulty.

—Bless this house and keep it safe by night and day. Bless the walls and chimney tall, Noah McNulty said. I bear news from the Patriarch of Constantinople.

—He carries news from the Patriarch of Constantinople, Pádraigh called over his left shoulder.

—What news? they asked from the bed.

—Eusebius of Constantinople wants your poetry translated into Greek.

This stirred a great interest in the poets, who had by now forgotten their Greek. Fame had eluded them. Fame, married to the wealth which they now had, could sate them. Some Patriarch, beyond Hannibal's Alps, had seen fit to have their poems translated. An Arabian, together with the oysters and lobsters, must have brought knowledge of them far across the seas from Ireland.

—Permit the messenger from Constantinople to enter, they called.

He entered and they recognized the figure of Noah McNulty.

——Throw him out, they said. He's a Baile man.

Pádraigh Gorm na Mara would have carried him to the cliff and thrown him into the winter sea, but Noah drew a parchment from his pocket, heavily embossed with a red cardinal's hat, cords and tassels and the seven keys to the gates of Byzantium.

——Will you not listen to the epistle from the great Patriarch, Eusebius?

——Stay your hold, Pádraigh, Tostach ordered. And let us see the parchment.

They looked at the medieval parchment. The calligraphy was monastic, the contents Greek.

——It's Greek to me, Tostach Joyce said.

——And to everybody else, Noah McNulty replied.

——Translate it for us, they said.

Standing beside the statue, by the candle light he read the translation.

> Illustrious Bards of the Island of Inis Orga, Greetings from the City of Constantinople.
> During the last month fragments of your poetry have been carried to our ports by sailors. One verse of Tostach Joyce's poem, entitled 'My Ass', has made its way into Greater Armenia. I have asked the Metropolitan of Baile, Noah McNulty, to have a poem by each poet of your esteemed school translated into Greek and carried to us at Constantinople in his ark, when it is launched. These poems will be copied by trained hands and circulated in Thrace and Macedonia. A contribution in gold for the purpose of finishing the ark would indeed be welcome as we are an impoverished church and cannot fund the venture.
> *Eusebius, Patriarch of Constantinople.*

——Recognition at last, they cried. And a recognition from Constantinople of the Scholars. Baile has looked down upon us. Dublin sends only peelers to raid our poteen stills, and London is not aware of our existence. Constantinople of the Golden Domes has recognized our worth.

——I'm always telling you to stand by the Church, Celibate Corcoran told them.

The letter was again passed between them and the red seal, the medieval smell, the ornamentation from remote monasteries testified as nothing else could that it was genuine.

Noah McNulty was invited into the ample bed. He drew
sheets of parchment from inside his shirt, together with an
ink horn and a quill.

——Who first for a translation? Noah asked.

——Me, Tostach Joyce said with great pride. The Greater
Armenians will certainly wish to have the rest of my poem.

He recited slowly, explaining the subtleties to Noah
McNulty, who with surprising speed translated it into Greek,
line by line.

When Noah had finished he passed the document to
Tostach Joyce.

——I don't know if he's got the internal rhyming correct
but the number of lines are right. Read it to us.

Noah intoned the poem in a nasal Armenian voice, stretching the vowels on high notes.

——It sounds as good in Greek as it does in Irish, they commented. And the strange wake music adds a dimension to it
which it did not already possess.

——All poems are chanted in Greater Armenia.

——So, we are taken seriously there?

——You are held in high regard in Greater Armenia.

Most of the poems were translated with great rapidity. One,
however, which was the last, proved more difficult than the
rest. For The Yellow Gunner, who had no interest in Greater
Armenia, continued to drink from his Greek wine cask. He
farted during the serious moments of translation and called
down black rain upon the See of Constantinople.

——Don't pay any attention to him. Were he not the poet
he is, he would have been dismissed from the school ages
ago. Perhaps his poem would have no interest to the Greater
Armenians.

——If the Patriarch of Constantinople is interested in an
Inis Orga ass, he's interested in a yellow bittern, Noah McNulty
said with sanity.

——I can't remember the poem, The Yellow Gunner said.

——You cannot trust a rake poet to remember his own
poetry. Lucky we have good memories.

From secondary sources they gathered the poem.

——Did I create that? and Damn, but that's a great line!
The Yellow Gunner interjected.

During the translation of this poem Noah McNulty wept
and laughed alternately, except once when he laughed twice
in succession.

——You weep and you laugh? the poets said.

——The poem makes me look back upon my life with both humour and pity.

Of all the poems Noah remembered only the 'Yellow Bittern'.

——It is now time to go, he said much later. The ark has to be finished and the poems carried to Byzantium. I'm sure you have not forgotten the request of Eusebius at the end of the letter.

——Concerning the gold?

——Yes.

——Pádraigh, bring down two creels of gold to the boat. We're dying to get rid of it, for the place is choked.

Noah McNulty dispensed a Byzantine blessing amongst the poets and followed Pádraigh Gorm na Mara who had a yoke upon his neck and his arms about two creels of gold. He sailed from the island, tacking before a contrary wind. Behind him a shroud of mist, like a judge's peruke, descended upon Inis Orga.

Well out of sight, he took the translations which were not translations at all and tore them into small pieces which the tide carried in a white line westwards. A sturgeon in exilic waters swept them into its craw. After this fashion they were carried to Constantinople and ended up as caviare upon the Patriarch's table.

Noah McNulty, with his catch of gold, sailed his boat for Baile. Some day he would sail again across these waters on his way to Byzantium.

Baile became aware of the new year, March old. Buds slit. The sky gained depth and extension. News of the great world came down the road on horseback, in Bianconi coaches and, from the far world, in ships.

During the winter they had complained of the cold, the rheumy wind, the absence of contact with London. Everyone had felt the pinch of poverty because no ship would brave the troubled seas from the south. Bone meal, hides, salted herring and pigs' feet had lain infertile in the warehouses. However, stories had trickled into the taverns; two Egyptians had been found floating by the pier, their fingers oyster-torn; on clear days French ships had been sighted off Aisling pier, though no decent ship had dropped anchor or furled a flag there in twenty years.

——What is happening under the cap of cloud? they had wondered.

——There is more going on there than meets the eye, for rarely do French ships brave these troubled seas in winter.

In spring the first hard news at last came into port in the body of a half-drowned French sailor. He was carried to Berwick Square by the city fathers and brought into the Versailles Room, warmed by French wine and his French translated by Madame Anna Morphy. The more the councillors heard his story, the more their wonder grew.

——Are you familiar with Tostach Joyce and Pádraigh Gorm na Mara? he asked.

——No, they told him. Island affairs do not concern us. They are barbarians and speak Irish.

——So you do not know the Celtic tongue? Pierre Le Clos asked.

——Fragments. But we are doing our best to forget it.

——Alors, at this very moment sea captains from half the countries of the known world are taking lessons in Irish.

——To what purpose? they asked in wonder.

——In order to buy the golden oysters, the red lobsters and the transparent liquid of the island.

They understood what Pierre Le Clos said, but they could see no sense in it

——Golden oysters, red lobsters, transparent liquid?

——Thanks to their power, our sainted Queen has conceived an heir, and he continued with his story.

Never before in their lives had they heard anything more extreme.

——And you mean to say that gold has been carried all winter through treacherous seas to buy Inis Orga lobsters, oysters and poteen?

——Oui, barrels of it. They have so much gold on the island now that they have driven the pigs and cattle up into the mountains and filled the outhouses with it.

——Of course you add to the story?

——No, by the bones of Pepin the Short, I do not!!

They sat and wondered. In their long years of trading they had not amassed a hundredth part of the fabled gold of the island.

——What do they plan to do with such amounts of gold?

——They have their plans. The poets of the island have already employed foreign scholars to translate them into Greek. The Patriarch of Constantinople has already received their works in translation.

——There are no poets on the island.

——There are.

——Tell us more.

——The whole economy of the island is run from the Great French Whore's bed.

——The what?

——The Great French Whore's bed, the largest and most valuable bed in the world.

It was too much for their firm minds and they said ——He's a French lunatic affected with salt water and exposure. His mind is fantastic. We'll bring him to the lunatic asylum.

They took Pierre Le Clos from the comfortable Versailles Room and brought him to the asylum. They knocked upon the door and the head keeper came out.

——Who have you here? he asked, looking at Pierre Le Clos.

——A French lunatic.

——He is the first French lunatic we have had here. What made him mad?

——Exposure and the sea. He imagines that Inis Orga is heaped with gold.

——He's the fourth lunatic who came to the asylum with the same story. Was he talking about oysters, crabs and poteen?

——No, oysters, lobsters and poteen.

——To my eye there is no great difference between crabs and lobsters. They all talk the same rigmarole.

The councillors realised there must be some truth to the stories.

——We have decided that he is only half-mad, they said and carried him back to Berwick Square.

They put Pierre Le Clos back into his comfortable bed and Anna was asked to translate the story again. He became petulant and only talked in short sentences, answering oui and non to their questions.

——We will have to pay a visit to the island, they decided. It is a pity to think of gold rotting in pigstyes and outhouses.

——If the great bed exists, then it should be in Berwick House, Madame Morphy told them.

——It is a bad time to put to sea or crew a ship.

——No matter. We must attack quickly. They may grow strong and powerful on the island. Anna told them.

——Agreed.

Anna Morphy called Rapparee Walsh.

——Do you think we could equip a ship and attack Inis Orga?

——Yes. There are a number of foreign sailors down at the

harbour bars. They could be thrown in jail and their release purchased by service. You can get guns and gunners in the military barracks. Lieutenant Forrester is given to venery.

—And what of ships?

—*The White Norwegian* is in the harbour. The skipper is in jail.

—He'll captain the ship.

The next night the jails were filled with the crew who would man *The White Norwegian*. They did not know what laws they had broken. Each one wished to return to his ship, lift anchor and sail from the evil-smelling town.

Anna Morphy lay with Lieutenant Forrester. He paid for his pleasures, which were rare, with half his regiment and two cannon guns.

—Perhaps when the expedition is completed you will have added another island to the British Empire. Think of Drake and Hawkins, she reminded him.

Three days were spent on rationing the ship and screwing the cannons into position. Marksmanship was practised upon a floating currach. On a fixed night the sailors were released and brought to the quayside, together with their captain, Natt Olsen.

Anna Morphy, dressed like a sea queen, told them of her naval plans.

—You will win a discharge if you sail this ship to Inis Orga. If you do not you will be thrown into the Burrows to rot. If, on the other hand, the mission is a success you will be invited to Berwick Square, wined and dined, and treated like kings in the Harem Room.

She ordered the crew to take up their positions. Then out through the gates of the military barracks, led by Lieutenant Forrester, marched half the Baile army. They stopped beside *The White Norwegian*.

—Do they understand the mission they are undertaking, Anna? asked Lieutenant Forrester.

—No. I'll leave you to address them.

He stood on a chest of Ceylon tea.

—The British Empire has been won, extended and maintained by small bands of brave soldiers who, in the hour of need, did not dread sea journeys, foreign shores or mountainous terrain. Tonight we are going to defend a threatened corner of that Empire.

They had been given a good cause. They marched on

board two by two.

——Hoist the sails, weigh anchor and head her into the wind, Anna Morphy ordered.

It was a cold night. The sea ran in ordered waves. No storm rattled the town windows or ran through narrow streets. Frost had hardened on the mountain of offal, sealing rot.

Anna strode the upper deck of the ship, her mind on gold and the Great French Whore's bed. She did not notice the path of the moon on the waves or the tranquil beauty of the stars.

——I wish we were at home in Baile, sitting by large fires, the municipal councillors said. Think of the gold. Think of the gold, they told one another. We can buy lands where cattle will grow fat.

Frequently they were sea-sick and wretched into the eternal sea.

They approached the double-backed island gestating in the sea. They passed Aisling pier, moved around the headland and sailed into Barra Bay, above which stood the cottage of Tostach Joyce.

——Lower the boats and make ready to approach the shore, Anna Morphy ordered. Fix the gun-sights above the house. Don't blow it to bits, for you might destroy the bed and scatter the gold.

Chattering with cold, the gunners pushed powder down the brazen muzzles, rammed home cannonballs and waited for orders.

——Fire!

The explosion rocked the ship and re-echoed in the hollow of the hills.

——Fire! she ordered again.

A nostril of flame rushed from the muzzle of the second gun. A cannonball hit the stack of turf behind the cottage.

——God Almighty! Gub Keogh said. The world is falling in. We are under attack from the British. What will we do?

——Do what the Irish always do. Retreat to the hills, Pat the Pagan advised.

The advice was taken. They jumped out of the bed, put on each other's trousers and shoes and streamed out the door and up towards the hills. They left behind the bed, the statue, the gold and Yellow Charles The Gunner. True to his Irish upbringing, Pádraigh Gorm na Mara also fled.

The Yellow Gunner thought that it was a bad dream which

brought on the vision. Redcoats burst in the door of the cottage, armed with swords and bayonets. They dragged him from his bed, broke his wine barrel and threw him into the ditch. They dismantled the Great Whore's bed, knocked a large hole in the gable, and carried it shorewards. They filled the gold into sacks and took it away. Six soldiers grabbed the statue and carried it away on their shoulders. By the bright, silvery light of the moon he watched a sea queen, lately come ashore, take command. The assault ended as it began.

The poets returned from the hills. They rescued The Yellow Gunner from the frozen ditch and carried him indoors. They looked at the holed gable-end and turned their backs upon it and gazed into the fire.

——We were better off miserable.

——It was too good to last, Cramp Carney told them.

——Only the stars are permanent. Fortune is as unreliable as the weather, and it skins the backside off stones, Mackerel Malone added.

——Everything, gone like the Tower of Babel, Stone Ryan said.

——Or the Hanging Gardens of Babylon, Celibate Corcoran added.

——Or the famous statue of Rhodes, Duck Flaherty added further.

——Or Tara's Halls, Rigmarole Rodgers added further still.

——I'll miss the bed, Tostach Joyce said.

——And so will we all. We'll miss the bed more than anything else. It's like losing a cow or a wife.

——The blackguards broke my barrel of wine. I wouldn't mind if they drank it themselves. As I looked at it pour from the barrel it was like looking at blood running from my vein. I can't live sober. I'd find reality hostile.

——All is not lost, Gunner, they told him. There are four-hundred barrels of Spanish wine on Aisling pier.

——Then I don't have to face reality.

——No.

They returned to their misery, a state in which they were no longer comfortable.

——We should march on the town, Stitcher Sweeney told them.

——We're not marching men, like Murtagh McMurtagh, who marches and marches and never goes to war. We are only famished and miserable poets, Kipper Padden told them.

——I never heard of a poet who was either rich or lucky,

and very few have enjoyed the comfort we enjoyed, Duck Flaherty said.

——It's a bad trade, they all agreed. We were robbed by a whore. Of what use is immortality?

They looked at the weak-hearted fire, symbol of their condition.

——We can wave goodbye to the bed.

The wind blew through the broken gable, the salt of the sea upon it.

——I think that we could get our bed back, Pádraigh Gorm na Mara told them.

——You have a simple mind, Pádraigh, they said. You would need an army to march on Baile.

——I was thinking of poisoning the whole population.

They looked up from their huddled position about the fire.

——You can't do that, Pádraigh. We will not have blood upon our hands.

——Well, we'll give them the scour! I'll loosen the bowels of the town.

——Is that possible?

——Possible and simple. I know the herbs on the hills. Some will cure and some will kill, and there are five that will induce the scour.

——Go ahead, Pádraigh, and loosen their bowels.

——I have seen Eastern towns, twice as large as Baile, brought low.

——It would be a fit revenge.

He went into the hills and gathered scour roots which he crushed and poured into a barrel and several bottles. It was tedious work, almost as slow as making poteen.

Anna Morphy sailed away from the island, happy with her success. She was now a rich woman and, in her own way, ruled Baile. Ahead lay the civilized lights of the municipal town.

Baile now felt secure. The statue stood in the Square, admired by those who knew the canons of Greek statuary. When Noah McNulty looked upon it in such an exposed place he knew that the time of desolation was ripening. It was no place for a naked woman. A god would come with his sickle and reap the hard barley of their sins; he would fire the stubble; four horsemen would ride a troubled sky. The Church found no fault in the statue; it was truly Greek and if it lacked modesty it carried harmony.

But it engendered sin in the minds of the drunkards who
reeled out of the pubs when the moon was on the mountains,
men who stained the pedestal and buttoned up their trousers
with uncertain fingers, potent only in their minds.

——Things were never better, the councillors said when
they sat in the panelled council chambers and fashioned small
codes. They were now rich men. They could build large
houses, send their daughters to Continental convents for
training and, maybe, furnish a ship. Money, like muck, was
best spread.

Anna Morphy had her bed. It stood in a crimson room, on
a carpet thick as a young meadow. Here Humper Donaghue,
after his congressional meetings, told her of his cairn of dung.

——I'll build it twice as high as the steeples. It will be half
as high as the sky and I'll cut out the figures of goats and
serpents and ravens upon it.

Upon Inis Orga the cloud cap was lifting. Its humped outline
grew firm and now by March it had all its dimensions.

Gold continued to pour into the island. They had more
than they ever needed even if life were to continue until the
crack of doom. Yet they were unhappy. No bed could equal
the Great Whore's bed and their statue had been carried into
slavery. They had been ill-used by the military power of
Baile. The hearthstone could have been broken in Tostach
Joyce's kitchen, it was so lonely without these things. Function
seemed to have failed. They went back to their fishing or
labour in the fields, trying to forget their winter in the bed
and their Greek experience. They found some small comfort
in the fact that their poems had been done into Greek and
were now familiar among the inhabitants of Greater Armenia.
Their minds were invaded with Celtic *ennui*, the worst form
of depression.

Tostach Joyce sat before the fire and looked into the
embers for some plumed bird. Pádraigh Gorm na Mara came
and went quietly, put a mug of tea in Tostach's hand, fed
him with fish and potatoes, and put him to bed at night.

——I'll never write again, he wept. Never again. All that I
have written is straw. The powers will never flow through my
mind again. I'm finished, Pádraigh.

——It will pass like the winter, this gloom upon everybody.

——It's a long winter when it is inside the mind. I feel as
dry as an old sally rod. There is no sap there anymore.

——The sap will come and there will be another poetic summer next winter.

——For one who once lived in a palace with white towers, I cannot understand why you endure this rock on the rim of Europe.

All his statements were fragmentary and charred with pessimism.

Pádraigh continued to gather his herbs and crush them with care. He poured the thick ooze into bottles and a barrel. Quietly and with African hate, he planned his revenge upon Baile. Two days before Saint Patrick's Day he was ready. He called the poets into Tostach Joyce's cottage. Some came in the door and others came in the open gable end, which had never been plugged. They gathered about the fire, their spirit-count low.

——I told you that we would surprise Baile, he said.

——You cannot surprise Baile, they answered with petulance. It has remained solid against attack for the last five hundred years. Besides, the English garrison under Lieutenant Forrester would round us up and throw us in the Burrows. A hundred Irish poets have perished there.

——It's possible, I tell you.

——It is not. Even Murtagh McMurtagh, with all his talk, would not march upon it, and he has sworn to destroy it and build a town on Tara.

——You are beaten before you go into battle!

——There is no use spilling good blood.

——Yet they tried to kill you. Have you no pride or no hate?

——Maybe we had last week. Maybe we'll have it next week, but at the moment, no.

——No blood will be spilt.

——We know, and we won't come. Let us live and die in misery.

——The back of my hands to the patriots of Ireland! I'll go myself. And he made to walk through the gable end of the house.

——Stop, Tostach Joyce called. I'll stand by you.

——And I'll stand too, Stone Ryan said.

——We'll all stand by you, we cannot let a blue man defend our cause and sit idly by.

——Explain the plans and give the orders, Pádraigh, Tostach told him.

Pádraigh held a council of war in the kitchen and explained.

——Each one will be given a bottle. His orders are to pour

the contents into a town well. Do you understand?
——We understand.
——And we sail on the evening of Saint Patrick's Day.
——A most significant time.

Saint Patrick's Day in Baile was celebrated with great pomp.
The councillors looked forward to it more than they did
Christmas.

To begin with, it meant that winter was over. Their ships
could move upon the seas again. Bone meal, pigs' feet, black
and white pudding, glue, leather, could be dispersed to the
four corners of the world. Commerce meant gold and all
standards were judged by the gold standard. Secondly, because
they marched through the streets, two by two behind the
temperance band, two by two in ermine and weighed down
with silver chains.

Their progress through the town was announced by the
sound of soft Irish airs, and Handel's music when they
entered the Protestant quarter. Blushing with respectability,
their souls saved, they marched up to the convent. They
knelt on *prie-Dieux* during the religious ceremonies while
Sister Monica skittered her beautiful fingers over the key-
board in search of sacred harmonies. After French wines and
nuns attending at each shoulder like ministering angels, they
marched away to the Black Brothers. Here they drank
Spanish wine, ate monastery duck and listened to doubtful
stories from the monks. They toasted Saint Patrick.

——He was a true Irishman, if ever there was one the
councillors told the Black Brothers.

——He understood the Irish and was as smart as polished
military buttons He had a quick mind, converting the Irish
in one day by plucking the national plant and explaining the
deepest mysteries by analogy.

——We might still be pagans and confused, if he had picked
a four-leaved shamrock, but luck was on his side. Maybe we
would be better off as pagans, one of the drunken councillors
commented and was carried to the monastery latrine where
he purified his mind.

With bellies full, and announced by the temperance
band, they called at the Protestant seminary. There they
met spare canons, were on their best behaviour, careful with
their English pronunciations, spoke civilly and forced mineral
waters down their gullets. The talk was serious and limited.
They listened with tolerance to pointless religious jokes.

——Saint Patrick was an Englishman, they told the canons. And were it not for the English, the Irish would be without temple or faith, still given over to the worship of idols.

In this way they patched the rift which might have appeared in the religious raiment of the town during the year.

Having finished their abstemious glasses of minerals, and suffering from induced sobriety, they retired to the Town Hall for a secular banquet. Everybody who was anybody, nobody or somebody was there. The oak room housed a few noble families, some of whom had their roots in Irish soil for over three hundred years; military men with insigniae; merchants; artisans; and Anna Morphy and her girls in white and chaste dress.

The night ended at Berwick Square when the convent and Protestant bells were hooded.

From Inis Orga, in three-quarter light, the fifteen poets and Pádraigh Gorm na Mara sailed for Baile. They carried the virtuous liquid. When they arrived at the quayside it was deserted. They fastened their boats to rusty iron rungs and stepped on to foreign soil. Almost immediately they felt nostalgia for the island. The stench of offal and horse manure filled their nostrils with its thick smell.

——Let us return home, Pat the Pagan said. I already hate the smell of the place. If we move far from the sea we might lose our way.

——We'll abandon the enterprise, Stitcher Sweeney added. It's a fruitless and dangerous undertaking by poets.

——Yes, we'll all return home, Tostach Joyce told them. It is easy to be brave upon the island. It is different on foreign soil.

The talk had carried them half-way up the pier. They had waddled after Pádraigh, complaining as they went. He put down the barrel and looked at them.

——Would you turn your back on me?

——We would.

Before they could further betray their cause he rushed along the pier, drew a knife from his belt and cut the currachs free. They limped away from their moorings like humiliated cattle.

——That was cruel, they told him. We are lost forever.

——If I hear any more moaning I'll throw you into the sea, or on to a heap of horse dung.

——You wouldn't.

——I would.

They reaped bravery from despair and marched up to Saint Anne's gate and knocked loudly. The porter heard the wooden sound beat upon his skull.

——Where are you from? he asked.

——Valparaiso.

——Are you Irish?

——Yes.

——Then if you're Irish, you are welcome to the town on Saint Patrick's night.

——I never saw a black Irishman before, he said as he opened the gate, looking at Pádraigh Gorm na Mara.

——You haven't looked hard enough.

They entered. Baile was a large place with many streets and, in places, three houses one on top of the other.

——Keep together or we are lost, they said to one another.

——Follow me, Pádraigh told them.

They walked through straight and crooked streets until they reached the statue in the Square.

——Now, said the blue man, we'll use this statue as centre. No matter how far you go into the town always return here. The best way to remember a street is to remember a public house as none of you can read the street names in English.

——Repeat all that again, Pádraigh, they told him

He repeated the orders and continued:

——Take the bottles from your pockets and, as you go through the town, pour the liquid into the wells and tanks. Mark X on the wells with your clay pipes so we will not repeat ourselves. Twelve hours later the liquid will make the town so weak that we can take what is ours.

——It's a bold undertaking.

——Follow all my instructions. Take lodgings in some small house, particularly in the quarter where they speak Irish. Don't tell anybody your business. Refuse water and tea or you will be weak for five days.

——That we will do.

They went in various directions from the statue, pouring the liquid into the wells and marking them with the bowls of their pipes. Then they found their way into small lodging houses where they slept two by two and backside to backside.

Pádraigh and Tostach went in search of the reservoir. There was a bar of moonlight upon it. They poured the liquid into the pool and waited. It coruscated for a moment and then went dark.

—Will it work, Pádraigh?

—Of course it will work. It is working already. It moves fast through water and will not be held at the filter beds.

—Will it taste?

—It has no taste.

They left the reservoir and walked through Baile on the evening of Saint Patrick's Day. The smell of gut-rot was strong in parts, the smell of horse-dung strong in others. Red lit, women in high windows invited them up the stairs.

—Rot carriers, Pádraigh told Tostach.

From dim taverns tobacco smoke issued on tallow light. The laughter was brutal and cracked.

—You could not trust the laughter of Baile, Tostach said. It has a bad ring to it, like the broken rim of a cart.

—Soon all noise will cease. There will be only the cry of anguish caused by scour as guts loosen.

—We'll leave them to their laughter. I feel the call of the island.

—So do I. In fact next year I think I'll try my own hand at composing a few poems. I won't feel properly insulated until I do.

—What will you write of?

—The curved back of the mountains, the clouds, the sea, falling rain and the sound of the wind up the chimney.

—There is fine matter there. I'm more of an animal poet, as The Yellow Gunner is a bird poet.

They forgot for a moment that they were standing where the smell from the offal and dung mixed equally. They were back again on the island, following island ways, locked into the ordered life of the tide and the recurring cycle of the seasons.

They followed a manure trickle through the streets and arrived at the Spanish Yard. They looked skywards at the Linen Hall of dung with its rising tower. They found a ladder and made their way on to the roof. Beneath them, as they looked into the twisted streets of Baile, people, head-big.

—Who's there? Who's there? Humper Donaghue asked from the half-finished tower.

—Two Inis Orga men.

—You have no right to be up here. You could slip on to the streets and that would be the end of you.

—We saw the wonder and climbed up.

—And what do you think of it?

—Bigger than anything I've seen in North Africa, Pádraigh

Gorm na Mara said.

—Is it bigger than the Church in Rome?

—Nearly.

—Well, it will be! It will be the biggest building in the world.

—I thought it was for export.

—It will be.

—You will scrape the moon.

Humper Donaghue grinned with green teeth.

—Someday I'll sit on top of the steeple and grab the tail of the young moon. I'll stab it with my fork and fix it to the steeple.

—It will bleed.

—It's equal to me. I'll skin it and from the hide make a garment for Anna Morphy which will shine at night.

—It's a large undertaking.

—I know, but the material is pliable and soon the work will be finished. I'll be remembered.

They said their goodbyes and made their way down the ladder and into the crooked streets. They walked until they came to a lodging house. Here they went to bed and waited for the tainted waters to take effect.

They had not long to wait. In the morning they all returned to the base of the statue. Following a familiar custom they took out their pipes, knocked them against the granite base, cut their tobacco thoughtfully and smoked it with reflection. Like the ancient monks, they thought of their homeland and hoped that they would soon return there. The wind directions were favourable for fishing. They became dreamy and a strange thing happened: their heads became invisible.

Baile did not take much notice of the wonder. The bowels of the town had melted. The inhabitants groaned and ran to the latrines. They rushed home to rush back again. Soon they lay upon the streets, groaning.

—A dose of the scour kills resolution, they gasped. On an occasion such as this even the rich have to admit they have backsides.

Upon that day no mercantile or muncipal business was carried out. Anguish was felt in high and low places. No plank was added to the ark, no revolutionary journal kept by Cormac McMurtagh. Had Murtagh McMurtagh marched upon the town that day he could have established himself without battle. He was, however, celebrating Saint Patrick's Week at his castle in the Barony of Skattery.

The poets surveyed the anguish and smoked their pipes. At midday they stirred themselves. They took the statue and carried it to the quay. They went to Berwick House and retrieved the large bed. They wondered much at the house and at the strange rooms, the whips and the costumes.

——As we say on the island, there is nothing that you can imagine that has not already happened.

The citizens watched them carry the Great Whore's bed through the streets, piece by piece to the quays. Then they took the gold which belonged to them and brought it to the Square. They made it into a large heap and left it to rot.

They had no desire to remain any longer in the town. They made their final journey to the quay. They took four boats and rowed towards home. At their backs the island was framed in gold. They rested the oars and looked round at the wonder.

——It looks like the land of eternal youth and we are rowing towards it.

They returned to the island, never to leave it again. After a week they were established in the bed and the gable end of the house had been walled in.

For his services to the island Pádraigh Gorm na Mara was made Taoiseach of Inis Orga.

——All we seek now, they said, is immortality.

Man and beast recovered in Baile. They decided never to make war upon the island again. The gold lust had been purged from the poets and some evenings as people looked out at the island from the quayside it became invisible for no apparent reason.

Stone Ryan looked at the two rocks upon Misneach Hill.

——There is a statue within either rock but I cannot see them clearly.

He took his currach and sailed out of Barra Bay. From the sea he considered the large limestone rock and the flat one beside it.

——There is no lady within the stone. No naked woman should be left standing on a hill beaten by black winds, or drenched by grey rains.

The wind caught a shallow belly of sail and the boat was carried slowly about the two rocks. His eye followed the running lines and he considered what was possible with limestone. No voice spoke to him out of the stone.

——He will go mad, Gub Keogh said. He thinks too much.

——No, Tostach told him. He will go mad when he goes dry.

Stone Ryan left the quiet sea and began to walk the small sheep paths meshing the hills. Sometimes he passed through the village before Aisling pier, his head bent, his face tight with thought. Eight women observed him pass. The long winter had brought no bliss to the sea village.

——Tostach Joyce should be banished from the island, Kate Keogh said. He draws the men from us. He hasn't done a hand's turn since that black man was washed upon the shore. The sea brings only misfortune.

——We might as well be in a convent, Lil Padden added. It's a hard thing spending winter alone in a bed. It's unnatural and no water to quench our fires.

——It is hard to be constant, Brigit Malone declared, not even the stars are constant.

——We will have to take the sea captains into our beds. They know the Eastern arts, Molly Sweeney told the court of women.

——We should all go to Baile and get paid for what we all want and live in the luxury of Berwick Square, Mag Carney suggested.

——It's too extreme. We will take in the sea captains, for they are clean men and scented, Peg Flaherty told them.

But Stone Ryan did not observe the sea captains make their way ashore. His mind was taut. He lost trace of day and night and rarely took food or drink. Flesh fell from his bones. His cheeks became hollow and gaunt. His lips wrinkled like a blue worm's body. He appeared for a while beside the stones on Misneach Hill, measured them, nodded, talked a little to himself and then, spectral and thin, disappeared again. He looked east and west at no singular thing. He was often seen on the dangerous cliff paths and wandering among the crooked slabs of the graveyard, scratching the puffy moss from the inscriptions.

——That man must be watched, Tostach Joyce said. He will take a weakness one of these days and fall off a cliff into the sea and that will be the end of him. Pádraigh, I'll place him in your care.

Pádraigh had many things upon his mind. He had sat in the pub by Aisling pier and listened to the polyglot talk. The island was infested with spies. Two of them, called Georges et Roger, were from Paris town. They told him they had come to paint the seascapes and the cloudscapes of the island. Each morning they set off with their easels and canvases strapped to their backs. They set them up at various corners of the island and accurately painted what they observed. When Pádraigh Gorm looked at the canvases laid out together on a bar counter he realized that they had mapped out the island, stone by stone.

——They have a complete map of the island, Pádraigh told the poets. No stone has been left unpainted.

——Surely they will not invade us? They have always come in the past as friends. It says so in the songs, and to prove their point they sang 'An Sean Bhan Bhocht'.

——Never mind what's in the song. The Emperor of France needs gold for the upkeep of his cavalry and his women. He has turned his eye towards Inis Orga.

——How much do you think we are worth? Tostach asked Pádraigh.

——You own two million gold sovereigns.

——That's a power of money!

——I know.

——What will we do with it? Gub Keogh asked. It is of no use to us and it will choke up every field on the island.

——We got the money under false pretences. We sold lies and foreigners paid for them.

——We didn't get it under false pretences, Rigmarole Rodgers said. The lie has turned out to be true. Haven't we heard stories from Arabia and Russia and Spain that testify to the power of the lobsters and oysters. Hasn't a pascha in Egypt, sterile for ten years, fathered forty.

——That's true, they admitted.

——And what have we heard about the King of Spain's mother? Hasn't she grown so young that she could be mistaken for her daughter's sister?

——That's true too, they agreed.

——So we have done well and done good.

——We must put gold to useful purposes.

——It's a scandal, what's been done with the gold; like the woman who used the first chest of tea ever washed up on the island for dying her petticoats, aren't some women in the village boiling spuds in golden pots, Mackerel Malone remarked.

——That's true, they agreed, Spanish gold pots.

——And the last I heard of Skully was that he was ploughing the land with a gold plough, and John Coogan cutting turf with a gold slane.

—True again, they agreed.

—And I saw Martin Reilly going down to cut grass with a golden scythe.

—Damn and blast the yellow skitter! Gub Keogh said.

—It has no cutting edge.

—Why can't we have things like they were in the old days, when there was hardship and misery? This island cannot endure without poverty.

—When did we last feel hunger? asked Stitcher Sweeney.

—About ten months ago, they all replied.

—And when have we been in need of tobacco?

—About a year and a half ago.

—And, now that we have tea chests of it, do we enjoy ourselves?

—Not as much as we did when we hadn't got it.

—Misery puts an edge on things, Rigmarole Rodgers said.

—Yes, we thought that the gold would end all our problems and instead it multiplied them.

—I wish the old days were back, Stitcher Carney said.

—But here we are, exposed to invasion, Celibate Corcoran continued.

—Will we be invaded? The Yellow Gunner asked.

—We could be, Celibate Corcoran said.

—Put the idea of invasion out of your heads, Tostach Joyce told them.

But then two Germans arrived on the island, Hands und Adolphe. They came to measure the island from side to side, they said.

—Why measure the island? Padraigh asked.

They told him that it did not appear upon German maps and until it did, it did not exist at all. They insisted that it was proper that it should exist.

Pádraigh Gorm na Mara followed them to the village pub and listened to their talk and marked their gestures. Hands und Adolphe were spies. They spoke of an invasion on the north of the island. He returned to the poets and told them of his discovery.

—They intend to have you talking German in three months. All cottages will be destroyed and German houses built in their place They also intend to make you work.

—That would be the greatest infliction which could visit us, equal in virility to the ten plagues of Egypt.

—But they would surely leave us our poetry.

—They have enough poetry in Germany. Where else on

earth is there a race of men who spend half the days of their
lives in a large bed composing poetry? What makes you think
the Germans would read your poetry?

——Leave us to our illusions.

They looked at the large bed; the fine French quilt, black-
holed with tobacco sparks; the humps and the hollows like a
drumlin landscape. It was a world of word and image and
illusion, the final island of their culture.

——Culture confined to a great whore's bed, Pádraigh
surmised.

All the thought and talk which had gone into the shaping
of a race for four thousand years and recorded on scattered
ogham stones, stained manuscripts, could be destroyed.

Already there were rumours from the village that their
women were consorting with foreign sailors. They had found
a purposeful use for gold. They now wore dresses from France
and mantillas from Spain. Another rumour stated that a tutor
of English had been invited to the island to teach them refined
English, and it was stated in another rumour that a coach
had been purchased in Cork and would be pulled by four
island asses.

——The women have gone over to pagan ways. Soon they
will know all the Eastern arts of love. Then they will develop
a taste for foreign wines. What we have stood for, and lain so
long in this bed for, may soon perish, Tostach said. Steps
will have to be taken.

There was monastic silence. In vision they saw their island
deserted, a lonely tide coming and going across Barra strand.
The houses were empty, their spines broken, docks and nettles
cropped on the thatch. The wind lamented the passage of the
poets of Inis Orga, as it lamented the passage of the men
from Troy and the memory of the loveliest woman in the
world. Their fires would be quenched, their hearthstones
broken, the poets scattered. They would wander through the
narrow streets of the towns, mumbling their poetry to themselves. In the end they would lie in graveyards, their names
anglicised upon tombstones.

——The yellow skitter has destroyed us, Cramp Carney said.

——I wish that we were wild geese, Rigmarole Rodgers said.
And we would fly over the grey sea and find peace in some
foreign place. ——I wish the white horse would come and take
us to the land of eternal youth. I'm tired and I'm growing old,
The Yellow Gunner said. ——It's the end of all we have known,
Pat the Pagan said.

——We were fools, running after gold and stacking it in barns. We have no guns to defend the island and we are unpractised in the arts of war, Tostach reminded them. There is only one wise and final answer to the question. Seeing that we can't put the gold to any use, we will have to shovel it over the cliffs of Doon into the sea where it will be shifted this way and that until it is lost for ever in the sand.

——It's a decision we have to take, Cramp Carney told them. We will be rich, unhappy and troubled with the gold, we can be poor and poets without it.

——I'd prefer to be rich and unhappy, Amorous Aynsworth said.

——No, Tostach is right, Gub Keogh told them.

——He is, they all finally agreed.

Having taken their own counsel, they called Pádraigh Gorm to the side of the bed.

——Pádraigh, put the creels on the ass, gather the gold and throw the yellow poison from the cliffs of Doon into the sea.

He creeled the ass, gathered the gold, and carried it to the top of the cliffs. Rolling up his sleeves, he took his large spade and shovelled it into the sea. The sun caught the coins in its light as they spun out and down, turning them into a constellation of stars. Then they splattered on the sea and were lost.

——It is a grand thing to be poor again, the poets said. It is satisfying to feel miserable. Misery is the kindling of poetry.

——It is a weight off my back, Tostach told them. For it was like carrying a bag of stones up a mountain, to build a cairn for a king, without ever getting to the top. It remains now to destroy the final rumour. This will be the end to gold or the chances of ever making it again.

——We know. We know. We do it with full consent and perfect knowledge and also knowing that it is a serious matter. However, we have seen the gold and handled it, and it will serve as an image in poetry.

——So, some prosperity has been drawn from it, Pádraigh told them.

With that he left the house in the miserable palm of two hills and made his way across the mountains to the shebeen. He ordered a dark pint and stood over it in a dark mood.

——You are in the black mood, Georges et Rogers said.

——A mood blacker than porter.

——C'est mal, c'est mal.

——Das ist nicht gut, Hands und Adolphe said.

Pádraigh Gorm na Mara, though purple, had always been optimistic. The sea captains and spies gathered about him, gathered about his black porter.

——You know what I discovered? he asked them.

——No, they said, always interested in something which might relieve island tedium.

——I discovered that the poets are liars and have taken advantage of me.

——Is that so?

——Yes. They have taken advantage of everyone. The lobsters have no power. The oysters have no power. The poteen has no power.

——How do you know all this, Pádraigh?

——I crept up on the house and listened to their talk. They laughed together and said that they had deceived the whole world.

——It was a substantial lie while it lasted.

——I know. Didn't I and half the world believe it.

——And what of our gold, Pádraigh?

——In a fit of rage I gathered it together and threw it into the sea from Doon cliffs. No man will ever lay his hands upon it now.

——What will you do next, Pádraigh, after being so deceived?

——When I have drunk this pint of porter, I'm going to return to the cottage and throw the poets and the Great French Whore's bed into the sea.

——Well, hurry up with the pint, they said angrily.

He poured the pint evenly down his throat, roared an African roar, and rushed from the pub.

Soon the island was abandoned by the foreigners and left to its ways. The only testimony to their presence was a series of French landscapes on the walls of Doolin's pub and some unfinished German maps. The island returned to its former insignificance.

Stone Ryan was unaware of the events which were taking place. He was still tangled in his mind. One night, as he was passing by the graveyard, he heard Paddy Goff staggering towards him. He was singing a sad, dark song. He listened to the words. Somebody had put old music to The Yellow Gunner's poem. He saw the song and the music in stone. It stood on the rim of Misneach Hill. The large rock carried the image of The Gunner and at his feet in the low flat rock the yellow bittern. He saw each line, each muscle, each sinew. The statue would stand there forever, in a bleak place away from warm hearths and human conversation. It would remind men that some are born lonely and wander through the world, foreign to its substance.

He returned to the cottage and slept for five days. Then one morning he took his chisel and mallet and set off in the direction of the hill. He worked for twenty days upon the limestone, fevered by creating. Out of the rocks he drew the man and the bird. On the highest hill Charles The Yellow Gunner looked forever upon a dead bittern.

——The statue will stand until time runs out, lonely above the sea, beaten both by wind and rain. It will tell all passing ships that the weak and the bent have great and remarkable spirits, he said.

He expressed no further wish to work in stone. The creative power, which he had possessed for so short a time, had been taken from him.

CHAPTER FIVE

The year shed its days. It was May in Baile, on Inis Orga and in the world in general. From the dung-steeple, half as high as the sky, Humper Donaghue looked down upon the countryside small and pleasant. The harbour was filled with foreign masts, grass was green in Berwick Square and small leaves were thickening upon the branches. Carriage wheels rolled over solid ground, carrying pomp and circumstance this way and that, moved by some civilised whim or other. Soft Indian breezes blew through the delicate porticos of the military barracks. The sun shutters were thrown open and Lieutenant Forrester looked out upon a well-administered landscape.

The wandering Raftery found himself on the shores of Lough Carra. When winter had set in he decided to stop at the house of Michael Quinn, the traditional fiddler. Each night, when the neighbours gathered in, Raftery recited his poetry or played the fiddle. When spring came and Saint Brigid's Day was well behind him he said goodbye to Michael Quinn and set out in the direction of the Barony of Skattery. He went by the small roads punctuated by warts of houses. By the beginning of May he reached the outskirts of Murtagh McMurtagh territory.

Skattery was seething with rumours of war. Every man was willing to die for Ireland — variously in the popular mind a firm-breasted woman in fetters, an unstrung harp, a ruined monastery, a bare hill dispoiled of its oak wood.

Murtagh knew that all the images were dangerous. Time for war had come. The tribes were restless. No hope could be expected from Spain and the wine upon Inis Orga pier was inaccessible. With the wine the war could have been waged vicariously. He stood alone. As Lord of the Barony he would have to give the order which would carry both him and his men into battle. Perhaps men would be killed and he had never seen a man killed, other than a cousin who had been kicked by a jennet. Worse still, he might conquer Baile. With the town in his possession he would have to lead his troops into further battles. Perhaps they would have to march across flat plains without a mountain where they could take refuge.

——The time was never riper, his adviser told him.

——I know. I know, he said brusquely.

It was too true. He knew at the back and at the front of his mind that if he did not march out through the castle gates and down the old bog road his kingdom would be lost to him.

——Let us put it fair and square to you, Murtagh, the chiefs said. We think you are an old sod and that you have no intention of ever going to war. We are tired of the talk and the stories. The young men will not listen to them any more.

——Is that so now?

——It is. They are tired of singing the genealogical rameis and the talk of help from Spain. They want your brother Cormac to lead them, or Flan, or Nealty.

——They would even be led by Nealty?

——They would.

Things were falling apart. The thatch was lifting off the house and no scallops to pin it down.

——War is a terrible thing, he said.

——It is, they replied, but there is nothing more terrible than the dull life of mountain and bog.

Murtagh spent wakeful nights walking up and down the penthouse floor of his castle, knocking his head against the rough oak beams, scraping the surface of his brain to discover some way out. But try as he could, there was no escape. He would have to become a reluctant hero.

He lay with his neighbour's wife, Nell, but she could not distract him from his fate. Fear swept through his whole corpus and his sinews melted. He was no longer certain if he could mount a horse or lead an army down a road.

——I'm afraid I'll have to die for Ireland, he told Nell one night.

——There was none of your ancestors but followed the call when it went out.

——I'm ready to die because I have no way out. It's a great pity Cromwell did not plant this bog when he came to Ireland. I might have had the good fortune to be in the Barbadoes today, cutting the tall sugar cane, a happy slave.

——That's no talk from the seed of Adam McMurtagh.

——My lineage does not lessen my fears. I have gout in my legs and there is too much lard about my belly. It's like a sack of stones slung from my shoulders.

——There is no way out. You will have to marshal the troops, or Nealty will take the barony from you.

It was a quiet night about the battlements. The winds had fallen to a whisper between bog-cotton heads. No traveller would be led from his path by erring lights. No portents could be read in the stars as they wheeled over the bleak countryside. He peered out each of the three windows, looking in turn north, east and west. The darkness brought no joy to his soul.

——A man is too old at fifty to go out fighting. He should be at home thinking of the battles he fought in his youth, he said.

——But sure you fought no battles in your youth, Murtagh.

——I lacked the opportunity. If I die, I'll leave the kingdom to no son.

——There will be a field full of bastards fighting for it.

——That's enough lip from you.

——It's true.

——It might be. But I don't want to hear about it.

He continued to walk up and down the room. In his mind he marched down the road to Baile a thousand times. It could not be taken.

——I'll have to get Cormac to start a diversion within the town. Baile will be taken from within and then from without. War is always won by surprise.

He knew that the young men were hatching plans which would overthrow him. His spies had told him that they were spreading rumours that he was bloated and old, that he was soft with pleasure and drugged with dreams. They spoke of overpowering the castle and throwing him in the dungeons.

——The young whelps, and some of them sired by myself. But I'll show them that Murtagh McMurtagh is battle-worthy, and not without plans. Have you the bed warm? he asked his neighbour's wife.

——I have.

——Well, move out of the warm spot and let me into it. Tomorrow, or the day after, I might be lying on a cold battlefield.

The next morning he buckled on his sword and went down

to the porridge pot. While he was ladling the gruel into himself he called his amanuensis.

—Are you ready for dictation?

—Yes, the amanuensis replied, taking vellum, ink and a goose quill from his scholar's satchel.

—Dispatch this letter immediately I have composed it.

The scribe crouched and prepared to take down Murtagh's words.

> Dear Cormac of the Bright Mind,
>
> The time is ripe. Already our army waits the command to go into battle. The military action must be fast and complete as the fields are nearly ready for ploughing. You will know that we are prepared to march when you see bonfires blazing on the hills. Next morning we will be on our way down the road, to Baile and the conquest of Ireland.
>
> As a reward for your faithful service you will be crowned King of the Republic of Munster, at Cashel in the presence of bishops, archbishops and a cardinal. Battle rages in our souls. We shall impose the ancient laws and customs upon the rest of Ireland. Hail and farewell until we meet upon the field of battle.
>
> Sincerely yours, . . .

The pen scratched to a halt.

—Give me a look at the letter, Murtagh commanded as he grabbed the vellum. It's fine writing, although I cannot read a line of it.

—I learned it from an old manuscript, the scribe replied.

—Will you illuminate it?

—Indeed I will, with small animals and fish, like the ornaments you see on old cloaks and bronze shields.

—Read it back to me, and in my own voice.

The amanuensis, who was also a professional voice imitator, read the letter.

—It's a well-worded letter. —It is, Murtagh, but you have already promised Munster to many of your chiefs. —I know, but in war a man has to make many promises that he cannot keep. Besides, I expect most of them will be killed. —Clear thinking, Murtagh. —Tell me, is that poet, Raftery, in the barony yet? —He is. —Is he stirring up the young men? —He is. They are nearly primed for war. —He's dangerous. —All poets are. —Send for him. He is an old enemy, stirring the barony against me. Poets start wars.

The messengers discovered Raftery drunk in a shebeen. He
had a bare-arsed servant-girl on his dry knee and was pro-
mising her immortality.
    —Remember my words! Remember my words, he said,
for tomorrow I'll have forgotten them.
    —You should sing of battles and not of love, they said.
    —Love is the great theme of poetry and war is of little
consequence. Things never change, victory in war changes
nothing. Someone will always have to cut turf and build
walls.
    —And what of our old and noble heroes?
    —More fools they. Their bones make fine lime for cattle.
    —You are a traitor, Raftery. You stir up young men
and then sit drinking in shebeens, cavorting with bare-arsed
servant-women.
    —Leave him alone, a faction said. Every poet in his drink
talks rameis. He has written good poetry in his time.
    A scuffle broke out. Bottles were broken on heads. Cud-
gels rose welts. Blood, more suited to the battle field than
the ale house, flowed.
    —Would that this were for Ireland, many cried.
    —He's a bad poet, voices roared.
    —No, others said, he's the best poet in Ireland.
    —No, said a traveller, the best poet in Ireland is Yellow
Charles The Gunner, and he lives in Inis Orga.
    They stopped fighting.
    —I never heard of him, and what great poem did he
compose?
    —It's called 'The Yellow Bittern'.
    —Sing it to us, after the old fashion.
    —I will. He put his elbow on the counter, after the old
fashion, hummed and then hawed, and sang the song.
    —It's a great poem surely, and better than Raftery's.
It will last forever. Who is this Yellow Gunner?
    —A small walker of a man, with yellow skin, who is
drinking himself into the grave.
    Raftery, peeved, left the tavern by the back entrance with
the messengers. He made his way on an ass to the castle, his
mind sour, professional hate in his heart for The Yellow
Gunner.

    —I want words with you, roared Murtagh at Raftery when

he entered the large hall. I'm tired of your lampoons.

——They were only meant as humour, my lord.

——Well, it's gallows-humour, and I'm strongly thinking of condemning you as a traitor.

——No traitor I, my lord. Just a travelling poet.

——Take him to the dungeon, Murtagh roared.

——Mercy, Lord Murtagh. I'll serve well the Lord of Skattery.

——Can you write poetry in my praise?

——Yards of it. Yards of it.

——Good. Have three yards of it for me tomorrow.

Untorched bonfires had been built upon the hills and Whistler Seán O'Farrell was ordered to commence his whistling, signs that the moment for battle was near at hand.

Hackett the Harper was taken from his corner and ordered to tighten the strings of his harp.

——What for? What for? he asked.

——We are preparing to go to war.

——A real war?

——Yes, a real war.

——But, sure I was never at a war in my life. All the wars I ever fought were inside my head, and that was a long time ago.

——You are ordered to string your harp, and that's final.

In the main room of the castle the table was heavy with food, red and yellow wine, and patriotism. Torches burned in brackets and black smoke, carried to the vaulted roof, lodged in a morose cloud. It was a night of music. Stories were told and rusty harps played. Murtagh danced jigs and reels with spirit and when the dancing was at its height he called for silence.

——There have been rumours of war and men have wondered if Murtagh McMurtagh was ready and prepared. Things were said about me by young men which should not have been said. My ability as leader has been called into doubt. Now I declare war! We'll march out of the castle to the sound of drum and harp, heads in the air, horses fed, and edges upon our swords.

——We'll march now, they cried. They drew their swords and banged them flatly on the table.

——No, we won't. The time is not ripe, yet, and we have a feast to finish. You cannot go into battle hungry, or at night-time.

——It's been ripening for the last forty years. We'll march now. Festy will lead us.

—It will be ripe tomorrow. We'll move into the wheat-fields of time and cut the corn of freedom.

—And we'll make bread out of it, they called, extending the metaphor.

—And feed upon it, Murtagh said, stretching the metaphor.

—You'll take us to the fabled shores of Clontarf, Murtagh?

—I will, but we will have to be careful we don't lose our way.

—And then to Tara, Murtagh?

—And then to Tara, where I'll be crowned king of Ireland.

—King of Ireland. That will make the King of Spain look up.

—You are the finest race on earth. Your ancestors were ten feet tall.

—So the songs say.

—And virgins will be able to walk from one end of the country to the other without being molested.

There was silence.

—I said, virgins will be able to walk from one end of Ireland to the other without being molested.

—Alright, they conceded, virgins will be able to walk from one end of Ireland to the other.

—Unmolested?

—Alright, unmolested.

—Of course the King will retain his divine rights.

—You're backsliding and devious, McMurtagh.

—Alright, virgins will be unmolested, even by the King.

They returned to drinking and pledging and dancing and praising and dividing land and counting cattle, and 'Ireland for the Irish', and 'Believe me if all these endearing young charms', and 'The harp that once, that twice, that three times through Tara's halls'.

—Light the bonfires on the hills, Murtagh called out excitedly.

Men rushed out of the hall with blazing torches. Over moor and dale they raced. They torched the bonfires. Soon they roared into flame and licked the night like the tongues of sensual sailors on the flesh of black women.

Noah McNulty saw the distant bonfires from the prow of his ark. It was the beginning of the end. He quickly set about nailing down the final deck-boards.

—Success depends upon clarity, Cormac McMurtagh told

his ten lieutenants who stood about his table in their revolutionary uniforms. Consider everything and break everything into tenths.

——That we understand, and we are in agreement with it, citizen, Higgins said. But are we ready for war?

——We are now ready. The plans are final. Each man knows his orders. It is time for the revolution. My brother, Murtagh, intends to march on the Baile. We must take the town before he does. There must be no confusion.

——We may be confused in our minds, Cormac, but there will be no confusion in our actions, Citizen Deegan said.

——The first building to take, he told them, is the asylum itself. This is poorly defended, from what we can gather. We will march out the side exit and approach the main door from the front. We will batter it down with a cannon gun. In the empty doorway we will read the proclamation in French.

——Agreed, citizen, they all said.

——Then we will convert the asylum into our headquarters. From here couriers will be dispatched to each tenth of the town. Every citizen will be asked to swear allegiance to the proclamation and the flag which will be dipped in the first martyr's blood.

——What martyr's blood? the lieutenants asked. There was no talk of martyr's blood when we began our preparations.

——You need martyr's blood for every cause. Somebody is bound to suffer some injury or other. As soon as blood is spilt on our side, steep the flag in it. And if there is none shed we will have to get some pig's blood from Shamble's Lane.

——I'll attend to that, Citizen Wallace said. If there is blood to be found, I'll find it.

——That is all, citizens. The dawn of the new millenium is nearly here. I expect that each one will do his duty. We will now march to the main hall and I will address the troops. And remember, the keepers think this is a musical concert. Never forget that.

With their cockades under their arms, their swords by their sides, the lieutenants formed a double row outside their leader's garret. Cormac belted his sword, arranged his cockade, went into the corridor and, taking the salute, walked between the double line with bent head as the ceiling was low.

Making an exit from the double line, he cried ——Gauche, droit! and off they marched to the assembly hall.

——Vive La République! he cried. Liberté, égalité, fraternité.

——Liberté, fraternité, égalité, they roared back at him.

——You have done a good job, Citizen Durcan, Cormac McMurtagh said to his lieutenant. You will get a medal for this when we strike medals. You will be able to show it to your children and their children's children.

After the clapping had died down he began his inaugural address.

——Citizens of the New Republic, the forces of battle are now drawn up. On one side stand the common people of Baile and the neighbouring townlands, starved, beaten, and in chains which they cannot rattle. On the other side stand the fat merchants of Baile, civil servants, the peelers and a handful of soldiers. They are the enemy. For too long have we been oppressed, for too long have we been downtrodden. But soon we will be at war and seen to be at war. We will press on until the final victory. Then we will build a state which will last for a thousand years.

——For ten thousand years, they cried back.

——For ten thousand, if that will satisfy you. And I expect that every man will do his duty.

——Will we be kings? some called out.

——Every man will be a king.

——And what about us? the women roared.

——There will be as many queens as there are women here.

——You have given us a great cause, Cormac. You have made us noble. We will free those in the Burrows, hidden too long in underground caves and fed upon porridge. Let the sun shine upon them. A fair deal for the lepers, the halt and the maimed!

——They will be all given a fair deal.

——You are a good man, Cormac. You have given us a cause.

——And now, chant the 'Hymn of the Republic' to me.

——We will, Cormac the Liberator.

They filled the hall with the thunderous peal of the new anthem.

> Citizens of the New Republic,
> Freedom's day is here.
> We'll break the chain which binds us.
> The future starts this year.
>> So build a state united
>> Where men can equal be,
>> As far as men are equal

Given human discrepancy.

They sang the hundred verses for Cormac. A hundred tears poured from each eye.

—I'll leave you with the anthem ringing in your ears. It will be sung again when we march through Baile. Let each man and woman return to his bed and wait for the day of liberation which is nearly here.

—That's the best concert ever put on here, a keeper said at the bottom of the hall.

—As long as Cormac McMurtagh keeps this story about his New Republic in circulation there will be no trouble from anybody. The concerts where everybody is involved will keep them all out of harm's way. Left to himself you wouldn't know what plan would breed inside his head, another keeper remarked.

Cormac left the stage. He walked down the hall to the thunderous applause of the inmates.

—We could be entering Paris, he told the lieutenant who stood beside him. Or after taking the Bastille.

He stopped in front of the keepers.

—Everything in order, sirs. The citizens of the asylum will peacefully return to their quarters. I will now inspect the military equipment.

—Go ahead, Cormac, they said. We will leave it to you. It is time for us to go to bed now. We like your fancy dress.

Cormac was now in charge of the asylum.

—I wish to see the guillotine, he told Lieutenant Wallace. —It has to be greased and oiled, but the blade is sharp and heavy. You need weight for a quick chop. —Will it sever a head with one stroke? —It should. It has severed head-sized turnips with caps on them. —Have you tried it on flesh and bone? —No, not yet, but we have a pig ready for the first run. —Are McGinty the Piper and Drummer Tucker ready? —Yes. They have been practising the martial airs. —Good. We must march into battle to the tuck of drums and the skirl of bagpipes. It puts courage into men. —We will go directly to the forge if you wish and examine the machine. We have prepared a full-scale guillotine ceremony for you, citizen.

They walked across the stone quadrangle where the insane at certain hours of the day walked in circles, wrestling with madness. Their revolutionary boots sounded on the stones and re-echoed from the walls.

In the forge the anvil rang out with the three ancient notes of the iron worker. Blake, the blacksmith from Lub, was beating iron crosses into pikes. About him sat the insane who could not sleep. They followed with glazed eyes the rhythm of his strokes and the constellation of sparks which shot out from the raw ore each time he beat upon it. The sparks died quickly in the darkness, after a brief life.

Perhaps during the duration of their existence they had spun to mathematical formulae. Perhaps, too, men had peopled them and had been scorched with the anguish of living and the tedium of dying. Thus one lunatic, comparing great with little, argued.

—Whoever thought of the idea of beating crosses into short pikes? a lunatic asked Blake.

—Dillon the Prayer. He was on his knees, praying at the old graveyard of the Large Sisters of Saint Vitas, before the iron crosses which mark the regiments of the dead, when he saw them flattened into pikes and dripping with blood of the enemy.

—Do you not think it desecration, ripping crosses from the ground? They mark the resting places of the dead and are like addresses on envelopes.

—The iron is being forged in a good cause. Taking time as the arbitrator of all things, the crosses would have rusted under the perpetual rains. In ten thousand years, the time given to the New Republic before it falls asunder, the crosses would have corroded. So it is just as well to take them and beat them into the emblem of the new state.

—I suppose you are right.

—There is no doubt in my mind about it. I will beat out the names of the nuns and imprint égalité, fraternité et liberté upon them.

They heard the military step on the cobbled yard. They donned their cockades and attended the arrival of Cormac McMurtagh.

—Is the guillotine ready? he asked brusquely as he entered the forge.

—Sharp and ready, Blake said.

It stood, bloodless, at the corner of the forge, a frame of oak timber on a platform of deal, and bladed with Toledo steel.

—Has it a good edge? Cormac asked.

—It has. I got Nestor the Scyther to sharpen it. He told me that it would cut a wet meadow or shave the hair off the face of a corpse.

——It will be good enough then for the revolution.

——Indeed it will.

——Has it wheels?

——Yes, and shafts so that it can be drawn from place to place as needed.

——Then it is better than the one in the book.

——Far better, because it can move.

——When it comes to striking medals I'll pin one on your chest, Blake, and you can show it to your children and their children.

——Merci, Citizen McMurtagh.

——It will have to be tested, Cormac directed.

——We have tested it on inanimate things, like turnips, but tonight we will see if it severs a pig's head, Lieutenant Wallace told him.

——What size collar does a pig wear? Cormac asked.

——Size twenty, I'd say.

——Well, that's about the size of the fattest merchant's neck. If it can cut through that, without lodging in a wind pipe or neck bone, it will serve the revolution well. Drag the guillotine into the square and we will execute a pig by moonlight, Cormac ordered.

——Orders are orders and when they are given they are to be obeyed, Blake said.

——Get asylum benches and we'll see how well the machine works, Cormac directed. And call the women out with their knitting.

They took the guillotine by the shafts and dragged it out into the square. It cast a sinister moon shadow. The new citizens of the future Republic took their seats and looked up at the blade caught by the yellow light. The guilty sow was led from the piggery. She carried heavy udders.

——She is the mother of all the aristocrats of the world, they cried out. ——What are her crimes? Cormac asked. ——She has sired vipers, they answered. ——And has she been found guilty before the people's court? ——She has been given a fair trial. The carriage of justice has been both impartial and democratic. ——Then she must die, Cormac said. ——Die she must, they all agreed in a popular voice. The shrewd-eyed sow smelt death. She rushed forward and dragged the halter from the hand which held it. ——She has escaped, Cormac roared. Follow her! She will mate and drop a litter of oligarchs. ——After her! they all roared. She will mate and drop a litter of oligarchs.

They followed the pig about the quadrangle. She twisted and turned and screeched. Finally she was caught and tied. She was brought before the tribunal and condemned in much the same words as she had been condemned before. Order and decorum were established.

——Sound the pipes and let us hear the tuck of drums, Cormac ordered.

McGinty the Piper filled the bagpipes with asthmatic wind. With bent fingers he drew away a sad wail from the stops. The sound mourned all those who had ever died in battle. It was sadder than the winter wind about a dilapidated castle or the shredded screech of a banshee limping across a marsh on the night when royalty or a young woman died.

Drummer Tucker drummed on the base of a whiskey keg. It was a soft beginning, which became firm and martial. When it reached marching pitch the beat was maintained.

Across the yard Drummer Tucker led all the revolutionary armies that had ever marched through Europe. After him came McGinty the Piper, lamenting the dead who never marched back across Europe. They stopped at the foot of the guillotine, its mouth open and ready to swallow the living. Hangman Casey held back its jaws with a rope and waited for the pig to be led up the steps and placed in position. Below him sat the women, an eye to the guillotine, an eye to the knitting.

——Tell me, are we at a church service? one woman asked. ——I don't know. Why? asked another. ——We seem to be sitting on church benches. ——Well, we must be then. ——Isn't it a great thing that they let us knit in church. ——It is.

The sow, slipping and reluctant, was dragged up the guillotine steps. Drummer Tucker sounded the tuck. The sow was now the enemy of the people. She was the landlord who had pressed pence from the poor, she was the councillors who strutted through Baile. To the better educated she was one of the aristocrats of the world. To Cormac McMurtagh she was the Great Dictator who had ruled the world for too long. They jumped to their feet when the drum tuck reached its dark crescendo. They called for the head of the victim. Hangman Casey released the rope. The Toledo blade, shark avid, rushed down the wooden grooves. The pig screeched. There was silence. The first blood had been spilt.

——We are now ready for the revolution, Cormac said as he looked at the pig's head in the sally basket.

They returned to their beds and awaited the glorious day.

Out through the gates of the Castle of Skattery on Monday
morning, listing to the left and listing to the right, marched
the soldiers of the twelve tribes led by Murtagh, his mind like
the barony, skattered. Beside him rode the spectral figure of
Hackett the Harper with fixed stare, a harp on his back and
knowledge neither of the event nor season of the year. To
Murtagh McMurtagh's other side rode Raftery the Poet on an
ass.

——Unfurl the flag, Murtagh ordered. The flag, which had
been furled for forty years, was undone by the wind. A harp,
holed, fluttered on threadbare cloth above the troops.

——To the left! he ordered at the crossroads.

The soldiers wheeled to the left; twenty men on horses,
fifty on asses, ten on jennets, six on mules and five hundred
on leather. The castle fell away behind them and then the
hills. They looked at the disappearing landscape.

——It's bleak out here, Murtagh said. I didn't think that the
world was half as extended as this. It is also flat in places.

——I always thought the world was furrowed with hills
and glens, and streams rushing through them, a soldier said.

——Apparently that is not true. There is no hill or wood
to take refuge in, Murtagh said.

——Then we will be fighting with our backs to the bogs,
which is a setback. Many a good man was lost in a bog hole,
and him only going to peer through the window of some
local beauty or other. Anything could happen when we are
in full flight, someone muttered.

——Who's talking of flight? Murtagh asked.

——The Earls flew and so did many others before us. There
are precedents, O'Malley said.

——Men get killed in battle, a soldier told them from his
position on an ass.

——It's no way to die. A man was born in a bed and meant
to die there. Better to die of cholera or famine than by gun-
shot or the sword, his brother on a jennet added.

——Stop bladdering, Murtagh said, or we will have a mutiny
on our hands. For forty years we have been preparing for this
battle and there is no returning now. On we must go or we,
and anyone bearing our name who comes after us, will never
live it down.

——We could be caught by a hard winter on our way to

Tara. If Baile is this far off and even further, then Tara must be a good many miles east of the northern direction we are taking.

Baile was still far away and the castle miles behind them. Down the small roads came men in twos and threes, some on asses, some walking. The army bloated as it marched. At noon they stopped at a stream stained by bog-rust. They drank a handful of water and a mouthful of oats. It was rough food for their stomachs, like sacking on the backside.

—Go easy on the oats, Murtagh told them. We have a long way to go and we can't be suffering from starvation when we reach Baile. We might be captured and carried in irons to the tower of London and shipped to the Barbadoes.

The soldiers munched the pre-battle food gravely.

—It is the same as eating sand, they complained. Why do we have to go into battle? Who wants to be King of Munster, or Ulster, or Leinster? We are not known in far away places and we will not be welcomed among strangers. Let us return to our wives and few acres, to where we belong and where we wish to be buried. We have come far enough and seen no enemy. Maybe he exists only in the old stories. We'll leave him there. We are not conditioned to fight in exposed places.

Murtagh considered the words. They had about them the comfortable ring of truth. They would return. They would invent the events of battle, bribe Raftery to sing about their deeds and all would be well.

—Mount, he ordered his horsemen, assmen, jennet and mulemen. The time is not ripe for battle. We will live to fight another day. To hell with Tara and all its towers. I abdicate as King of Ireland.

—And I'll leave Munster to the Munstermen, a voice said.

—And I'll forfeit the crown of Leinster, another voice added.

—We'll leave the land to those who have it. We'll live and die in peace with everybody and return to the old ways, they all agreed.

They executed a turnabout manoeuvre and started back in the direction of Skattery. The skies however, which had been growing black, discharged. Thunder, brooding for three days, barked. Lightning crackled and flashed, plunging bright roots into the earth. The figures of the warrior dead appeared above them and mocked their retreat.

—We better continue on our way to battle, Murtagh said. They swung about and headed north. The rain and thunder passed. The clouds lifted and the sun shone upon their reluctant progress.

So on Monday evening Murtagh and his army arrived at a crossroads with good fertile land to the north, east, west, south. Here a small town had been built. It was their first contact with the Roman order of civilization. They marched into the middle of the town and those who were mounted, dismounted.

——Do we march on, or pitch camp? Murtagh asked them.

——Pitch camp, they called. We will fortify ourselves with bread and porter and play cards.

They inhaled. There was a strong smell of porter on the air. They followed the smell, which brought them to Miss McCuter's pub.

——Time to rest before battle, they said, a bird never flew wingless into war. It would be a pity to go over to the other side with no taste of drink on the breath. The man who made time made plenty of it and, if we don't get to the fight tomorrow, then we'll get there the day after. Why should one carry gold into battle?

Raftery entered the pub with them. He sat on a high stool and told Miss McCuter that he was a poet and that if they did not get good drink he would satirise her. Fearing that his verse might blister her memory, she served the drinks as they were called. When the moon was bright on the mountains they were all drunk and not sure if they were coming or going to battle. Raftery had already written a victorious poem for them. There was no one under the low rafters who did not receive honourable mention. They carried scars which were not fatal but were nevertheless immortal. By midnight Murtagh was crowned King of Ireland and those petty princes, who had so lightly abdicated their crowns under the harsh light of reality, had fought and won them again.

On Tuesday morning they marched out of the town, having asked for direction from an old travelling woman.

The War Office was only too well aware that Murtagh would finally be pushed into battle. During the winter many dispatches had arrived in London. It was evident that part of the Empire was in jeopardy. Let one barren, unmapped section secede and the whole might fall apart.

——Why are we called from our country estates? a Member of Parliament asked in the House of Commons.

——It's the Irish Question again, the Prime Minister told

them.

——Not the Irish Question again, they groaned. We thought that we had that kingdom finally conquered. It says so in *The Illustrated News*. The Empire is at peace. These are golden times.

——Gentlemen, the Prime Minister continued, we are not at peace. We are not at total war. But a large moth is eating the corner of the raiment of our Empire. His name is Murtagh McMurtagh and he is preparing for war. As far as I know, he may be engaged in battle and carrying war into settled towns.

——Murtagh McMurtagh? they repeated. Never heard of the fellow. Spell it out.

The Prime Minister did. There was some doubt as to the correct pronunciation of the name.

——Parley with the devil. Parley with the devil. Give him what he wants.

——We cannot. He speaks Erse and none but a few speak Erse.

——Send troops then, Prime Minister.

——We have neither troops nor battleships. They have been dispatched to the East.

——Then bring back the Chelsea Pensioners. They may be old, and some of them may be very old, but, by God, they have stout hearts. Stout as oak they are.

They agreed that the veterans were as solid as oak. And so they were drawn into regiments and ordered aboard the old oak ships. Old sails were hoisted and off they sailed to fight the old, old wars.

A fair wind carried them down the Thames, past Greenwich. Under the auspices of a good wind they turned south and then west. They sailed along the south coast of Ireland, then headed north in the direction of Baile. The weather, moody for three days, took a bad turn. Rheumatic drizzle began to fall. Old Peninsular wounds opened. Festers ran. The ships' surgeons amputated limbs with the aid of rum and tar. Many of the veterans died and were buried in the dark

idiosyncratic sea, where their bones would never rest but
would roll this way and that, moved by the shift and shuffle
of the tides.

One ship was carried on to uncharted rocks. They tore
the hull. A strong wind cast high waves against the wreck.
The masts cracked. The planks snapped. Marauded by the
sea, it heeled over and slipped under the waves. But the
mariners and the old soldiers were brave to the very end.
They sang 'Rule Britannia, Britannia rules the waves'. They
died in a good cause and had no cause for complaint. They
were remembered later when a little peace to record history
came between the wars. Each name was cut out in stone on
some plinth or other, somewhere in a public park, somewhere in England.

Some ships did get through. They sailed on towards Baile.

Murtagh stood on a rim of hill, looked on the town and said
—I didn't think it ever existed. I have heard much talk about
it but I thought that it was only talk.

—It's big, one of the soldiers said, and it looks permanent.

—It would be a pity to disturb the good people going
about their business, and not one of us properly dressed. We
have neither the way nor the manners to enter the town.

—I want none of the poor mouth now, Murtagh told
them. Don't we all know that we have the blood of princes
running in our veins. Can't we trace it beyond the flood.

—Maybe we can, the soldiers said. But who will believe
it or who wishes to hear?

They looked down upon the town filled with life and
activity. About it stood the walls holding back the wilderness. Each wall carried a stout gate and above each gate stood
a soldier in red, well-armed.

—Now that I see it, Murtagh told his troops, I don't
think that we will be ever able to take it. If we had cannon
guns to train on the walls and breach them, we might stand
some chance, but as it is we stand no chance at all. That is a
considered military opinion.

They all agreed and nodded their heads wisely. They had
come a long way, seen a lot, and it was time to return.

Murtagh said —We'll go home. We could lose life and limb
in an assault on the town, and at the end of the day we would
have nothing to show for it. We will return someday, after a
natural disaster, when the walls have cracked. Then the time
will be right. But now we must return home and prepare.

It was wise counsel, counsel which they all wished to hear.
They turned their backs on the town and were set upon the
road home when they heard the wail of bagpipes.

——I know that sound, Murtagh said. It's McGinty the
Piper, who was put in the asylum for bad bagpipe playing.

——It's unmistakable, sure enough, they all agreed.

——By Balor's black and evil eye, Cormac the brother has
started the revolution!

The mind of Cormac McMurtagh was cool, satisfied, content.
He sat in his room, entered some thoughts in his diary and
reflected. Nothing could go wrong. The plans were as perfectly worked out as the answers to Euclid's geometry. Each
citizen knew what to do. He sipped his red wine.

At half nine on Tuesday morning, to McGinty's music,
the inmates of the lunatic asylum dressed for the revolution.
They stood about him in their colours. Each lieutenant
commanded ten men and they in turn ten more. Every
battalion contained a hundred and this gave them a fighting
force of one thousand, one hundred. Each soldier was well-
shrouded, carried a weapon of some type or other, a blanket
to wrap himself in against the frosty nights, and ten fistfuls
of conglomerate gruel to sustain him over the first three days.
A tin mug dangled from each military belt. Behind the
columns of armed men stood the women with their knitting.

At ten to ten the outhouse doors were thrown open and
the brazen cannon was drawn from the dark, secret interiors
into the sun. At five to ten the forge door was opened and
the guillotine drawn by a mule was moved into position. At
ten the unbloodied standards of the revolution were unfurled
and fluttered in the breeze. At nine minutes past ten Cormac
McMurtagh appeared on the balcony.

——Vive La République! he shouted.

——Vive La République! the crowd roared. The revolution
was on.

McGinty, his bag of wind under his elbow, squeezed. He
drew revolutionary music from the chanter. Drummer Tucker
tucked his drum to a measured step. The step was taken up
by the lieutenants and soldiers. The women took it up on
their knitting needles.

——They are well-drilled, a keeper said. You could almost
send them into battle.

Through the side gate the revolutionary troops marched
and around the front of the building. They brought with

them the cannon which they directed at the large, oak door, stuffed it with powder and rammed home a ball.

—Fire! Cormac ordered.

The old cannon exploded, killing Gunner Kelly. But the lead ball, turnip-centred, shattered the oak door.

—Dip the flags in Gunner Kelly's blood, for he died in a noble cause, Cormac told them.

The blood of Gunner Kelly, aloft on fluttering flag, gave body and flavour to the revolution.

Citizen Murtagh stood, as he had planned, at the battered door and read out the Proclamation of the New Republic. It was at this point that the keepers realized that they had a real revolution on their hands. Immediately Cormac had finished his statement the soldiers of the revolution charged the door and poured in through the main entrance of the asylum.

—Take all the keepers prisoner, Lieutenant Wallace said, and incarcerate them in jail number one.

—Do you know something? Citizen Cuffe said to Citizen D'arcy. This place is familiar.

—Yes. I could swear that I've been here before.

Citizen Cuffe pointed at the prisoners. —And to prove that I was here before I would swear that I have seen these faces.

—I suppose you are right, and he did not moider his head with further cuestions. The revolution was on and he was enjoying it.

The keepers however sat impounded and bound.

—There is more to this than meets the eye, one said. —Well, enough has met my eye to convince me that this is no concert, another remarked —The guns were real. —And so was the guillotine.

—March to the walls and march to the pier, Citizen McMurtagh ordered. Open the Burrows and release the halt, the maimed, the lepers and those condemned to death.

Drawing the cannon and the guillotine behind them, the revolutionary army marched through the town. A small contingent broke from the main army and stormed the barrack walls. They seized the English soldiers and carried them to prison number two to await constitutional trial. They threw the oak gates open and retired.

From the hilltop Murtagh McMurtagh and his irresolute army watched the gates swing open.

——Advance, he ordered, as there is nothing else we can do.

They advanced on the town expecting it to disappear from view. But it remained firm and rooted. They marched through Saint Anne's gate and looked about them.

——I declare this conquered territory, Murtagh McMurtagh roared, but the inhabitants did not understand Irish. He called his amanuensis to his side.

——Will you tell the bellman to ring his bell and tell the town that it has been annexed to the Barony of Skattery.

——What's in it for me? the bellman asked.

——Eight acres in Clare, Murtagh answered.

——Fair do's, the bellman said and walked through Saint Anne's parish calling out the news of the invasion.

——Is it Murtagh McMurtagh, the barbarian from the back of beyonds? the crowds asked in a whisper.

——The very same, the bellman told them.

The news spread through the quarter. The merchants surrendered to Murtagh.

——By the powers that be, Murtagh said, but we made our first conquest without shedding or drawing blood. We better throw up ditches and guard this place against my brother Cormac for he is mad and cannot be trusted. From now on there is a price upon his head, forty cattle and eight hundred acres of land in Meath.

News of the invasion of Baile, from within and without, soon reached Anna Morphy.

——What invasion? she asked an apprenticed whore who carried the news.

——I don't know, but Murtagh McMurtagh is in control of this parish and his brother Cormac is taking control of the rest of the town. Cormac has just proclaimed the town a Republic.

——Go on.

——This room is in the Irish section of the town, subject now to the Brehon Laws. The north side of Berwick House is in the French part and I suppose that we will have to speak French when we go across the stairs.

——How many girls know Irish? Anna asked.

——Many of them know the greetings in Irish and the drinking cheers but beyond that, very little.

——We'll get them to repeat the few words we know, or we are lost. I understand enough myself to get by. Tell me, what sort of a man is Murtagh McMurtagh?

—A devil for the women, they say.

—That's to our advantage. Now assemble the girls in the dining room.

—We will all be destroyed, the whores sobbed.

—Stop the whinging, Anna told them. Can any of you play the harp and sing Irish airs?

Two raised their hands.

—Good. Find two harps. The rest of you, get Irish costumes with shamrocks and round towers embroidered on them. Every one assume virtue. Our only hope for the moment lies in virtue.

There was a flurry of women through the rooms of Berwick House in search of traditional Irish costumes.

When Murtagh finally reached the Square he found a traditional *feis* in progress. On the platform sat two harpists, dressed like the women in the poems, playing jigs and reels for a group of comely and black-haired maidens with pear breasts and fine legs.

—A little field of Irish ways and customs in the middle of a foreign desert, Murtagh said. We'll bring them to Tara and install them in the halls.

—Musha, Anna Morphy said in the best Irish she could command, if it isn't Murtagh McMurtagh, the great man himself, and the uncrowned King of Ireland. A hundred thousand welcomes to the soles of your feet, and I hope the road rose with you wherever you came from.

—It rose in parts and fell in parts, Murtagh said, and who is the fine woman I'm talking to now with fine breasts and a brave look in her eyes?

—Áine Ní Mhurchú, fine gentleman, who puts the hospitality of her house at your command.

Murtagh saw the half-eaten apple of evil in her eyes, and he said —Sure, I'll leave the fine girls to entertain my soldiers, and maybe you would have a bit to eat and a drop to drink and a bed for a weary warrior?

—Indeed I have. It's rarely that a king comes to visit me.

They went indoors and Murtagh ravaged his food.

On the previous night a slave ship from Africa had anchored in the bay. Cormac decided that the slaves should be liberated. The revolutionary army, led by Tucker's drum, marched down to the pier. The ship was overpowered. Cormac delivered a liberation speech. It was translated into Swahili by Koola Akibu and bawled down into the yawning hold of the fetid ship. The slaves were released.

——And now, men from Africa, let us take the town of Baile, Cormac ordered.

The revolution proceeded to a fixed plan in the rest of the town. Tribunals were set up. Before these were dragged the rich to account for their wealth and the tyranny they exercised over the poor.

——Death to them all, the people cried when the rich were dragged before the Republican judges.

——Tyrants breed tyrants, and either we take off their heads or their nuts. Better their heads. This was the general logic of all the judges.

And so Tuesday, the first day of the revolution, was spent securing territory and rounding up the enemies of the people. When death did come, as it comes in all wars, it did not come upon the first day but upon the first night.

The first major battle was called the Battle of Anna Morphy's Whore House. When night fell the battle-weary went in search of wine and pleasure. Anna called her whores together and gave them firm instructions.

——Be prepared for invasion in two languages. The Irish will come through the front door and the Republicans will use the back entrance. You all know the words égalité, fraternité, and liberté? Well, use them on the French side. On the Irish side use the words cead míle fáilte. We must keep one leg in a French bed and another leg in an Irish bed, and our hearts out of both of them.

At eleven o'clock there was a knock upon the front door.

——Is this the house of ill-repute, mam? the King of Leinster said when the door was opened.

——It is, Anna Morphy replied. And who may you be that would be calling at this late hour, and the small innocent stars of the night shining down on your fine brave form and finished limbs?

——The King of Leinster, mam.

——Well, it is you that is welcome a thousand times, and a thousand times a thousand times.

He walked in the door followed by eight big, shy men, wonder-struck at the lavish habitation and the lights.

——It is surely like a king's palace, the King of Leinster said. The carpets are as high and thick as good grass.

The whores put on their Irish costumes and came to greet the soldiers, calling ——Fáilte, fáilte, ceád míle fáilte.

They sat the men about oak tables snowed down with food and drink. Harp music was played to them which melted their hearts. They began to weep on the whores' shoulders and, later, between their breasts.

——We are off to save Ireland and maybe die for it. Look well upon us, for you may not look upon our like again. We fight that a virgin may be able to walk from one end of the country to the other without fear of molestation.

——A right and a brave cause. I suppose you'll have us all in convents? Anna said.

——Yes, there will be convents everywhere.

——But not tonight?

——Not tonight, Anna.

——Well then, we'll get the harpers in to play until the morning. We'll dance the surface off the floor. You can remove your trousers to make the dancing easier but carry your swords in case of attack.

Sword-belted, and in longjohns stolen from the workhouse and smuggled out of Baile, they danced across the floor. Soon they found the longjohns too heavy.

——It's like being in the land of eternal youth, one of the young men said.

——We were mad to stay in Skattery so long, listening to the yarns. Win or lose the battle, but I'm not returning.

They all went off to bed, inconvenienced by sword belts.

Anna left the King of Leinster to his military dreams and went over to the Republican side of the whorehouse. It too had been invaded. Naked soldiers, wearing Republican cockades, wandered about the rooms, roaring slogans.

——And remember, Citizen Wallace said, carry your weapons by your side, for the fox, Murtagh McMurtagh, might attack us in our hour of weakness and anguish.

——We'll do that.

——Now, call in the women until I have a look at them, he ordered.

They came in.

——Get them to put on their clothes, he said, they all look the same to me and make choice impossible.

They did and he made his choice.

Harmony might have held and order reigned and the battle never taken place had not Citizen Wallace, by mistake, entered a Celtic urinal.

——Vive La République, he grinned to a naked soldier.

——What are you talking in a foreign language for? the

soldier asked in a foreign language.

They looked at each other for a moment. Then they rushed from the urinal simultaneously, shouting in their respective languages.

——There are spies amongst us, Citizen Wallace cried, disguised in nakedness. Find them and slaughter them.

Panic filled the hallways and the rooms. Untrousered, but with swords in hands, the Irish assembled.

——There is more here than meets the eye, roared the King of Leinster. We are surrounded by enemies in coloured hats. The Republicans are in the back part of the house.

——Run for it, a soldier suggested.

——Indeed we won't, the King of Leinster said. 'Tis the only bit of Ireland worth fighting for.

——It's true. We'll protect the women against the French.

——I hope none of you are feeling weak?

——Devil a one of us, sir. We'll chase the buggers out of the place. We'll have no Republicans here.

In the meantime Citizen Wallace, cockade askew, rushed into the back of the house with the news that the Irish had pitched camp in the front of the house.

——Fall into line. The first battle for the Republic is about to begin. We cannot leave the ladies of Berwick Square to the rapacious lusts of the Irish. Some may die. Some may not. It will be all in a good cause. This is our greatest hour.

Grasping their swords and pikes and sickles, they attended the orders of Citizen Wallace.

——Keep your cockades fastened to your heads. Lose them and you become enemies. ——Is war necessary? a voice asked. Is it necessary to die before our time? ——If you die you'll be remembered. ——I don't want to be remembered. ——We better go to war because if we stand here we'll catch our death of cold. It was the best reason they could find. ——Into battle then, Citizen Wallace roared. ——Liberté, égalité, fraternité, they roared in reply and charged through the building looking for the Irish enemy.

The fortunes of war moved this way and that, like the comings and goings of erratic tides. Whorehouse ground was taken and retaken. Standards were raised, to be torn down again. The sound of political slogans woke the sleeping city of Baile. They gathered in the streets and looked up at the lit windows. They followed the silhouettes of battle. They roared encouragement to the factions.

——We have the people behind us, Citizen Wallace said.

——We cannot let the people down, the King of Leinster told his troops.

. Much blood and wine was spilt. There was blood on the carpets and wine on the walls. Two died, not by the sword but by falling down three flights of stairs. Eventually the Republicans were flushed out the back door. They carried their naked wounded and their drunken dead.

Murtagh arrived late for the battle.

——Why are there many wounded but only a couple dead? he asked.

——We had forgotten to sharpen our swords, Murtagh. Had they been sharp it would have been a different matter.

——We have taken our first place, Murtagh said. It is as well-appointed as any palace in the old stories. I'll set up my headquarters here.

His view of Anna Morphy in her French transparencies weakened his strong heart. She was like a woman from the dream poems encountered in the imagination but not in reality.

——Will you marry me? he said directly.

——Have I any choice?

——When Murtagh McMurtagh throws his eye on a woman, her choice is already made. We will marry while there is battle gore on the flagstones. Send for the Wandering Spanish Friar and let him bind us for better or for worse.

The soldiers went in search of the Wandering Spanish Friar. They found him muttering to himself, his face towards a graveyard wall.

——Will you wed two who are wanting to be wed now? they asked.

——I will. I will. I suppose they'll have to be wed if the urge is upon them.

——Will it be legal and binding and in Latin? they asked.

——Oh yes. The Latin mightn't be grammatical, but it will be binding.

They led him through the Irish tenth to Berwick House. There was great excitement among the soldiers and the whores.

——She's getting a grand man, the soldiers said.

——He couldn't have picked a better woman, the whores replied.

Murtagh, dressed in his Celtic cloak embroidered with shamrock, waited for his bride.

In her room Anna Morphy put on her wedding dress of

Irish linen. Her hair cascaded down her back as hair does in the dream poems.

—Do you think I'm taking the correct step, marriage is a very serious business? she asked the maids-in-waiting.

—In these confused times it's the only one to take. If the Republicans overpower this tenth, the marriage can be annuled. And if they do not, then it is better to be married than single. Murtagh McMurtagh might take you to Tara and crown you Queen of Ireland.

To bagpipe music she made her way down the stairs, and to bagpipe music they were bound and knotted in doubtful Latin by the Wandering Spanish Friar.

—Take her now to the regal bed, Murtagh, and give us a king, the chieftains said.

Shoulder-high they carried both to the bridal bed in the Byzantine Room. The soldiers helped Murtagh off with his leather trousers and laid him between the sheets. Later the ladies came and prepared Anna Morphy for the King's bed.

At four o'clock that night, and to the sound of the Protestant church chimes, their union was cemented.

French order reigned in the other nine-tenths of the town. Dispatches, carried by couriers on the backs of asses, were brought to and from the asylum at precise intervals. Names and dates were inscribed in large books. Property and riches were relocated.

When news of the wedding arrived at the headquarters of Cormac it unsettled the tranquil state of his mind.

—He'll lose his head for this I swear. He has stolen our Goddess of Reason. From now on there is a price on his head. The first man to bring back his tongue on a plate will get a hundred guineas.

—But no man will have money in the New Republic, someone reminded him.

—We'll give it to him and then we'll take it back. It's not illegal to carry money yet.

In his hovel Humper Donaghue heard the rage and the roar of battle. Already the town was filthy with the dung of horse, ass, jennet and mule. He had tried to push his barrow through the streets but had to return on account of the confusion. The streets of Baile, once compared to the streets of Bath, were choked and filthy. A rage burned in his soul and he damned revolutions and rebellions. Only a torrential downpour would rid the place of the slime and the dirt and the horsedung. The revolutionaries might even tear down his building on him. He was, however, determined to ring his bell. He would beat out its new voice with a shovel. He would tear down the scaffolding and let the world see the great building he had completed.

Noah McNulty knew that the end was nigh. His congregation gathered about him when the storm of the revolution broke.

—Has the time of the deluge arrived? they asked.

—Yes, he said. The time is at hand. Carry the final planks to me and I'll nail them in place.

The ark stood finished, a huge timber box of a ship which had never been tested on any sea. The animals who had chewed the cud in the nearby paddock were herded together, tested for sex and driven up the long gangway by the shepherds of Byzantium. Bags of potato seed, oats, cabbage plants and turnip seed were stacked in the hold. The knight and his lady's tombstone was carried on board, as well as the bag of grinning skulls.

—Is everything in order? Noah asked.

—Everything ark-shaped and in good order.

—Then throw aside the gangplank and we'll abandon ourselves to whatever will happen.

All through Tuesday night in the belly of the ark, which had taken many years to build, they waited for the rains to fall which might carry them away from the town to Byzantium.

By three o'clock in the morning Baile was quiet.

The sun rose on Wednesday. The revolution was a day old. It looked down upon the new world with a sceptical eye, as it had looked down upon a thousand revolutionary dawns. It moved up the sky at an unexcited pace, tipping the mountains with purple, the offal heap with red, the dung cairn with green, as was its usual habit.

But to the eyes of Cormac it was very bliss to be alive. The revolution had succeeded beyond his maddest dreams. Baile had already the form of all future towns.

There was one dark blot on his plan. Murtagh had stolen the Goddess of Reason, married her, and still held part of his kingdom. The Wandering Spanish Friar, whom he would have made an ambassador, had shackled them together.

A messenger arrived at midday on an ass. He carried news of serious import.

——It is reported, Citizen McMurtagh, that Murtagh McMurtagh is to be crowned King of Baile in two hours time and Anna Morphy will be made Queen.

——Death to royalty. We will carry them to the prison and guillotine them some day next week. What this revolution needs is the death of a king and a queen.

Murtagh could not determine when the kingship and the queenship of Baile entered his mind. But on the morning after his first night with Anna Morphy he called the kings of the provinces of Ireland and stated that he wished to be crowned King of Baile with Anna Morphy his Queen.

——We have no crown, Murtagh, one of the petty princes said. ——How long does it take to make a crown for a king and a queen? ——Ten days. ——Ten days is nine days too long. Are there any old kings and queens buried in these parts? ——We don't know. ——Find out.

They brought a councillor into Murtagh McMurtagh's presence.

——Are there any old kings and queens buried in these parts?

——I don't know, but a story has it that a Spanish king and queen, in transit to South America, were taken by cholera in the Bay of Baile and buried in the Black Brothers' cemetery.

——Then dig them up and carry their crowns to me, for they won't be needing them any more.

——But nobody knows the exact spot. One story points to one corner, or other, and another still to a third, which leaves only one corner, and that has been indicated also.

——Well then, dig up the four corners and the middle and bring the crowns to me.

——It's a sacrilege to dislodge the bones of the dead, the princes told McMurtagh, and we don't know what evil will befall us as a result.

——Let every man of Saint Anne's parish get a spade and start digging.

The bellman went through the streets and announced the new command. The grave-diggers assembled in Berwick Square, former men of distinction and former men of no distinction. They were marched by the King of Munster to the graveyard and ordered to dig.

——And if you find any accidental treasure, like rings and

things, bring them to me for I have orders to collect them. Put the tombstones along the left ditch, and the sacks for the bones along the right ditch. We will bury all the bones later, for we must have respect for the dead.

Two hundred men footed two hundred spades into the earth. It was good earth, brown, not too light, and rich in lime. By midday they had reached the dead. Skull after skull was spaded into the bags, but no crown was discovered. They passed beneath the bone level. Here the earth was dark and heavy.

—There could be no bones here, they said. It is too deep. Nobody would dig this deep, even to bury a king.

—Keep digging, the King of Munster said. All the old stories are true.

They dug. The old stories were true. They found two skeletons carrying gold crowns. They were carried to Murtagh.

—They were probably relatives of mine, he told Anna.

—It's a grand thing to know that I married into royalty.

—By this marriage you are directly related to Adam, who was the first McMurtagh.

—I didn't know that.

—You learn something every day.

—Go and get that Wandering Spanish Friar and see if his Latin extends to the crowning of kings, he called to one of his soldiers.

The Friar was led back to Berwick House. By the time he reached the steps he had discovered enough Latin with which to crown a king, and a queen. A Byzantine throne was brought down to the main hall. It gleamed with a thousand lustrous baubles. Beside it was placed a French commode of the eighteenth century. Sitting on these thrones, surrounded by the royalty of Ireland, to the sound of ancient harps and to the solemn intonations of both classical and unclassical Latin, Murtagh McMurtagh and Anna Morphy were crowned King and Queen of Baile.

Their reign was neither long nor very prosperous. While the parish of Saint Anne was carousing, the revolutionary forces breached the ditches and assaulted the drunken soldiery. The battle was quickly lost and quickly won. King and Queen were taken in chains to the asylum and locked in prison to attend the whims of the revolutionary council.

The revolution was a success. The town was in chaos. Cormac's soldiers took to the taverns and began to drink old French wine. They paraded through the streets and welcomed the midday of the New Republic which would last for ten thousand years.

——The guillotine, the guillotine, we have not tested the guillotine.

They found it in a field. They took the shafts and dragged it into the main square.

By evening the first head had rolled into the large sally basket. The first head was followed by a second and a third, until they lost count. When the basket was full and would carry no more, they called off the executions.

Humper Donaghue decided that the time had come to hang the bell in the tower and sound its broken voice over the town. It would be the bell of the revolution. He shovelled the horse dung away from the bell of bronze. He polished it with rough sacking, hoisted it on his back and carried it skywards. He hung it on the girder he had prepared. Taking his shovel, he brought the iron down on the bronze. It rang out in broken voice over the town and told the world that the revolution had been a success.

To the chaos, confusion was now added. In from the pier of Baile, and through the town gates, marched a small British expeditionary force, the remnants of the Chelsea Pensioners. They dragged several cannon behind them. They marched directly to the military barracks, billeted there and trained their guns upon the asylum. They commenced to fire. By evening the walls of the asylum were breached. Cormac watched his Republic fall about him. He ordered his troops to assault the barracks but they lost their way. The remaining section of his army turned against him and refused to obey orders. They drifted back to the asylum square, from whence they had marched so bravely. With them they dragged the blood-drenched guillotine.

——What is this I see? Cormac asked, when he looked down from the balcony.

——We want to return to the old ways. The world is not ready for your revolution. We want neither liberty, nor justice, nor friendship. We want a bed and something to eat and the warders to give us orders. We have no other desires.

——This is treason.

——If this is treason, then this is what we wish for.

——Fire on the people, he ordered his lieutenants.

——We will not turn on our own.

—My lieutenants have deserted me, he cried and, taking a blunderbuss, aimed it at the crowd. Vive La République, he called, and fired.

—To the guillotine with him. He's the cause of all our miseries.

The lieutenants took him and dragged him from the balcony and down the stairs and out into the yard.

—He ordered the guillotine to be made. Now let him die by it, they cried in communal condemnation.

—No! Not the guillotine. Let me like a soldier fall.

But they dragged him up the steps of the guillotine, tied his head in position and let him roar for a minute.

—Vive La République, he called out, again and again. Vive La Rép . . . were the last two and a half words he uttered.

The sharp blade, blooded by the revolution, rushed down upon him through oaken ruts. Cormac McMurtagh died and with him the revolution.

While the execution was in progress Humper Donaghue looked down from his tower upon the disorder and confusion of the streets and discovered how they might be cleaned. He looked at the dam and the water behind it.

—If I could loose a lower block in the dam, then a large stream would rush through the streets and carry the filth and the blood to the sea. All would be clean again.

He came down from the tower, took a large sledge-hammer and went to the foot of the dam. He looked up at the high wall built by Ali Haffa of Egypt. It held back the strength which turned the wheels of the mill, and upon which the prosperity of the town depended. He lifted the sledge-hammer and brought it down upon a block of granite. Hour after hour he chipped at it. Darkness came but he continued his work inwards. By morning he had almost finished. His body was tired and his limbs ached. It was dark in the tunnel and he was in a long way. Suddenly, the rock face in front of him collapsed and the rush of water carried him out into the light. It rushed past him into the streets.

—The town will be clean again, he said to himself.

But as he spoke the dam above him began to shudder like a large animal awakening from sleep. It bulged out and exploded. It carried all things with it. The factories crumbled. The offal heap, sheltering within it Olc Mór, fell apart. Berwick Square, with all its splendour, fell before the rush of water. It carried away the cairn of dung upon which Humper

Donaghue had lavished so much care. The slender Indian walls of the barrack broke under its pressure. On it rushed, carrying buildings large and small. It reached the asylum. It gushed through the corridors and rooms, pushing out the walls and shouldering up the roof.

——The deluge has come! the deluge has come! Noah McNulty cried.

He watched the wall of water rush towards him. It lifted the ark above the rooftops and carried it seawards. Quickly he raised the square sail and the wind took the ark over settling waters. It moved past the floating bodies of Murtagh McMurtagh, Anna McMurtagh (nee Morphy), headless Cormac McMurtagh, Humper Donaghue, the Wandering Spanish Friar, the Large Sisters of Saint Vitas, Rapparee Walsh, Sagittarium O'Connor, the councillors and the less important corpses of Baile.

But when the ark was safely at sea it sprang a leak. Then plank after plank snapped. The sea poured in, drowning those in the ship's hold. Noah McNulty climbed the mast. The sea had no mercy. The ark destined for Byzantium slid beneath the waves, carrying with it the last survivor from Baile.

The poets of Inis Orga, stirred by some inner knowledge, had stood all day beside the statue of The Yellow Gunner and the bittern, looking towards the town. There was little they could do when the dam burst and destroyed Baile which had hoped to survive for ten thousand years.

——There is no end to wonders, Stone Ryan said. Everything gone in the winking of an eye.

——And to think that they looked at the sunrise this morning, not knowing that they would never see it sink behind Inis Orga, remarked Stitcher Sweeney.

They looked at the corpses and the wreckage upon the sea beneath them.

——The sea will grind them all to sand, and people will forget that Baile ever existed because they left no story of any greatness behind them, Gub Keogh said.

——Their flame was easily quenched. It was snuffed out in a moment, Mackerel Malone added.

——Ah, they were a hard people and they never looked upon life under such images. No great thought ever stirred in the depths of their souls. They were too bent on the colour of their gold, Tostach Joyce said with finality.

They turned from the disaster and looked at the sky beyond the island. Evening was coming on. It had flooded the sky with gold. Off towards the south the evening star gathered strength. The poets and Pádraigh Gorm na Mara followed Tostach Joyce down the rim of the hill, like monks coming home from the fields. Below in the cottage, under the warm blankets of the Great French Whore's bed, the golden wool of immortality was waiting to be spun.

WOLFHOUND PRESS FICTION

The best in Modern Irish Novels and Short Stories

KELLY: A NOVEL MICHAEL MULLEN

A fabulous, entertaining romp around Ireland, full of Swiftian invective and vicious satire. It is both funny and serious, an absolutely great read.

'. . . its ancestors include *The Crock of God*, the grotesqueries of *Finnegans Wake*, even *Jurgen* . . . ' *Punch* Jan. 1982. 'Michael Mullen belongs in the company of the Celtic revivalists . . . *Kelly* is most successful when it is at its most satirical.' *TLS* '. . . he is genuinely sorcerous with words' *London Times.*

'Unbridled inventiveness and Rabelaisian prose' *Irish Independent.*
'. . . it is certainly the funniest fantasy I've ever read . . .' *Fantasy Today (USA)*

Hardcover £6.00

NOVELS

FAMINE LIAM O'FLAHERTY

'*Famine* is worthy of its author and of the whole corpus of contemporary Irish fiction . . . it is the kind of truth that only a major writer of fiction is capable of portraying . . . this is the simplicity of flesh, blood, starving bellies, anger . . . it breathes verbal and structural mastery.' *Anthony Burgess, Irish Press*

. . . *The Brothers Karamazov* or *Fathers and Sons* . . . Balzac's *Les Illusions Perdues* . . . the *Faust* legend . . . *Tom Jones* . . . Manzoni's *I Promessi Sposi* . . . *Don Quixote* . . . It is to this company that Liam O'Flaherty's *Famine* belongs.' *John Broderick, Irish Times*
Paperback £5.95

THE ASSASSIN LIAM O'FLAHERTY

'O'Flaherty genius is at its best in registering mass emotion . . . there are some vivid sketches of Dublin's slums and night town.' *Irish Times*
Paperback £2.95

SKERRETT LIAM O'FLAHERTY

Based on actual events which took place on the Aran Islands at the turn of the century, this book tells the story of David Skerrett, and his rebellious defiance: 'I defy them all, they can't make me bend the knee.'

'(O'Flaherty) has all the potential of becoming a matrix for the yearnings of another generation . . . I found the reading of it beautiful.' *Neil Jordan, Hot Press*
Paperback £3.25

THE BLACK SOUL LIAM O'FLAHERTY

The book's primitive force, comparable to that of Emily Bronte, Hardy and Lawrence, shows an artist whose work embodies what Yeats calls an energy that is genius.
Hardcover £6.00

THE WILDERNESS LIAM O'FLAHERTY

'In addition to its central allegory *The Wilderness* is rich in symbol . . . a direct confrontation with the conflicting forces of his own creativity . . . One of the few really important Irish writers of our time.' *Irish Times*
Hardcover £7.00

THE ECSTACY OF ANGUS LIAM O'FLAHERTY

'. . . is it only in the shadow of a myth that men peer into their apparent fear of women . . . lyrical . . . erotic . . . O'Flaherty can effortlessly create the eternal freshness of myth.' *Irish Press*
Hardcover £4.50

SHAME THE DEVIL AUTOBIOGRAPHY LIAM O'FLAHERTY

'The finest autobiography of this century . . . a work of genius' Ulick O'Connor, *Independent*. '. . . it is never less than damnably readable'. *Irish Press*. '. . . passionately intense . . . it is a remarkable book'. *Sunday Tribune.*
Hardcover £8.00

SHELL, SEA SHELL LIAM LYNCH

Liam Lynch celebrates in this 'novel of sexual wound' the triumph of individual lives trapped in horrendous public and private circumstances.

'Shell, Sea Shell is a superb piece of writing, a real tour de force. It is as concentrated as lyric poem . . . profoundly, satisfying in its acceptance of humankind and in its awareness of beauty.' Irish Democrat
Paperback £3.50

THE KYBE HUGH FITZGERALD RYAN

An imaginative historical romance set in North County Dublin in the Ireland of Napoleonic times. A lively, engrossing narrative.

'As with all good novels, it's the little incidental details which provide the unmistakable ring of authenticity.' Sunday Press
Paperback £3.50

IN NIGHT'S CITY DOROTHY NELSON

'In what must be one of the most remarkable of all Irish novels, Dorothy Nelson's In Night's City, the taking of risks is not an option but a necessity for all the taboos of human relationship have been broken and the novel is a powerful document of survival.' The Linen Hall Review, 1984
Hardcover £7.50

THE CLOUD OF DESOLATION SAM BANEHAM

'I was . . . firmly in his grip impressed by the sheer density of his narrative and the skill with which he explores the eccentricities of 'Utopian' administration'. Observer. '. . . the bleak future he conveys is nastily convincing.' Irish Times. 'A clever and imaginative essay into apocalypse fiction; a thought provoker by an author well worth reading.' Sunday Independent
Paperback £3.75

HERMITAGE MERVYN WALL

'. . . a compelling fable of the Ireland of yesterday and the day before. Mervyn Wall knows his Dubliners . . . and many of his creations . . . or re-creations are rivetingly accomplished.' Irish Press.
Paperback £3.75

SHORT STORIES

VOYOVIC, BRIGITTE and other stories by NIALL QUINN

'A remarkable, indeed scarifying vision . . . the whole book . . . has the effect of astonishing originality . . . What joy it is to find a new Irish writer who is utterly unparochial' . . . *John Jordan, Irish Independent.*
Paperback £2.95

DAVID'S DAUGHTER, TAMAR MARGARET BARRINGTON

Introduced by William Trevor, these are stories about father/daughter relationships, social and religious prejudices, love of animals; the integrity of women, and the relationships between women and men.
Paperback £3.00

PADDY NO MORE: Modern Irish Short Stories
William Vorm, Editor

'This for me is very much what literary vitality is about...' *John Fowles.*
Paperback £2.95

SOFT DAY: A Miscellany
PETER FALLON AND SEAN GOLDEN

'One catches from it the success story of Irish literature, and its warm certainty of continuity.' *Irish Press*
Paperback £4.20

IRISH MASTERS OF FANTASY
Peter Tremayne, Editor

Stories by Bram Stoker; Le Fanu; Maturin; Fitz-James O'Brien; M. P. Shiel; Lord Dunsany. Biographical essays.   Portraits. Illustrations
Paperback £3.50

SHORT STORIES BY LIAM O'FLAHERTY
(The Pedlar's Revenge and Other Stories)

'This book is great value . . . he is always for the under-dog, for courage, for liberty . . . most effortlessly hits the stars.' *Sean O'Faolain, Irish Press.* 'A satisfying choice . . . compels belief . . . never wavers for a single phrase.' *Times Literary Supplement.* 'A worthy representation of an unflinching lyric writer.' *Sunday Times*
Paperback £2.95

FESTIVAL of

The discovery of the Great French Whore's bed,
and on it a man from Africa, afloat in Barra Bay initiates
this *Festival of Fools*.

On the island of Inis Orga, double humped like a
Bactrian camel, and in the town of Baile a rollicking saga
develops that gives us Madame Anna Morphy, whorehouse
keeper; Noah McNulty, zealot; Murtagh McMurtagh,
uncrowned King, and his brother Cormac, lunatic
revolutionary. Supported by a hilarious cast
of eclectics they drive their zany
ambitions to apocalypse.

Beneath the earthy comedy, subtle allegorical satire
slides and slithers. Prejudice and pretension are routed.
No sacred cow (or bull) is spared — all are driven
to the slaughterhouse.

In a dazzling *tour de force* Michael Mullen balances
the horrific and the hysterical. His robust inventiveness
never flags. Mullenland has arrived.

Enjoy the blend of farce, fantasy and satire, but do not
be complacent — its barbs will soon pierce you!

FOOLS

WOLFHOUND PRESS

68 Mountjoy Square, Dublin 1.

£3.50 Paperback ISBN 0 86327 051 4   ISBN 0-905473-91-4 Hardcover